DON'T JUDGE ME

DON'T JUDGE ME

LISA SCHROEDER

SCHOLASTIC PRESS | NEW YORK

All rights reserved. Published by Scholastic Press, an imprint of Scholastic Inc., *Publishers since 1920.* SCHOLASTIC, SCHOLASTIC PRESS, and associated logos are trademarks and/or registered trademarks of Scholastic Inc.

The publisher does not have any control over and does not assume any responsibility for author or third-party websites or their content.

Library of Congress Cataloging-in-Publication Data available

ISBN 978-1-338-62854-8

1 2020

Printed in the U.S.A.   23

First edition, November 2020

Book design by Yaffa Jaskoll

For everyone who has ever felt small or inadequate—**you are enough.**

And for everyone who has bravely stood up to make the world a better place—**thank you.**

DON'T JUDGE ME

CHAPTER ONE

Sometimes I like to imagine what it must be like to have a large family at dinnertime. Probably a little chaotic. Loud. Maybe messy. But I bet if there are school forms to sign, the parents hardly read them. Or if one of the kids doesn't feel like talking, no one even notices. That must be nice.

Since it's just the three of us in my family, my parents *always* notice if I don't feel like talking. Some days it feels like a giant sign with neon lights flashing at me: TALK TO US, HAZEL! TELL US ALL YOUR THOUGHTS AND FEELINGS!

The lights were about to start flashing at me across our Friday night dinner table at Ruby's Diner. It's a favorite place of ours, with booths covered in old-fashioned red vinyl and a counter with round stools, where people sit and drink thick, creamy milkshakes. I love strawberry the most because they use real berries. The waitresses wear pink dresses with aprons while the men wear black pants, white shirts, and pink bow ties. As my dad likes to say, "It's very retro."

I'd brought a book along with me to read, because I much prefer reading to talking. I was finishing up an old favorite, *The Adventures of Pippi Longstocking*. It's always been my comfort book, and since starting middle school, I've *really* needed some comfort. I discovered Pippi when I was little thanks to a statue of her that stands in the park in front of our city's library. When Mom told me about Pippi, I'd wanted her to find the book and read it to me. So she had. And I fell madly in love with the girl named Pippi Longstocking.

Pippi doesn't care what anyone thinks. And she's so unique. She loves to sail the seven seas, she wears her two braids in such a way that they stick straight out from her head, and she can lift a horse with one hand.

For my birthday that year, Mom got me my own set of Pippi Longstocking books. It's hard to know how many times I've read the original book, but if I had to guess, I'd say around thirty.

While I read my book, my parents talked about some problems Dad was having with a coworker. But once our food came and I set the book down, the questions would start. They always did. And I needed to show them something that was probably going to infuriate them, especially my mom. I'd brought it with me because chances were good Mom wouldn't make a scene in a public place.

The waiter gave us our food and as soon as he left, I picked up my burger and took a bite. I was starving. But the texture was all wrong. I forced myself to swallow, set it down, and took a long drink of water. My face must have given away my disgust.

"Hazel, are you okay?" Mom asked. She'd ordered her usual soup and salad. Meanwhile, Dad worked on his bacon cheeseburger like he hadn't eaten in five days.

"It's not well-done," I said. "I don't know if I can eat it."

Dad wiped his mouth with his napkin. "Then let's send it back."

"No," I whispered. "That's so embarrassing." I picked up one of the crinkle fries that came with it. "I'll just eat the fries. It's fine."

"Sweetie," Mom said with her warm smile. "He asked how you wanted it and you said well-done. If they didn't give you what you want, it's okay to ask them to make it right."

Sometimes I wonder if becoming an adult gives you superpowers, one of them being the ability to do most anything and not get embarrassed by it. Well, unless you're Pippi Longstocking. Something magical must have happened to her as a baby. That's my guess. But take my dad, for example. He has no problem taking out the trash wearing his robe if he's forgotten to do it the night before. Really, Dad? You're okay with the entire neighborhood seeing that old, ratty green robe you've had for at least a hundred years?

And then there's Mom. Nothing fazes her. Last weekend we drove down to Salem and went to Macy's. As we browsed a rack of sale shoes, she burst out laughing.

"What?" I'd asked. "What is it?"

She'd pointed at the shoes she'd worn. "I was in such a hurry, I didn't pay attention to what I was doing. Look, I'm wearing two different shoes."

They were the same style, but one was black while the other was navy blue. She works at a coffee shop, which means she's on her feet all day. When she finds a comfortable pair of shoes that she loves, she often gets multiple pairs in different colors. Seems boring to me, but whatever. Another superpower adults seem to have is that boring doesn't bother them. At all.

"Well, hurry," I'd whispered. "Buy some new ones and put them on, before anyone sees."

"But I'm not really finding anything I like. Besides, hardly anyone will notice, and if they do, well, I bet every woman in here has been so exhausted or rushed at some point, they've done the same thing."

I couldn't believe it. She was okay walking around with two different shoes on her feet? In *public*?

"Can I go look in the teen section?" I'd asked. Yes, I admit, I didn't want to be seen with her.

"All right. I need to stop at the cosmetics counter. I'll be there in ten minutes or so. Stay alert. Be safe." Her favorite four words make me sigh every time she says them.

Now, before I could stop her, Mom had waved down the waiter. I stared at my glass of water like it provided all the answers to the universe. If only!

4

"I'm so sorry," the waiter said. "It must have gotten mixed up with someone else's. I'll have the cook make you another one right away."

"Thank you," my dad said while I muttered, "Sorry."

"Oh, nothing to be sorry about," the waiter said. "We want you to be happy!"

I wanted to say, "I'm in sixth grade. Do you remember what that was like? Happiness seems about as hard to find these days as the lost socks that magically disappear in the laundry."

"So, how was school today?" Mom asked.

I'd been in middle school for about a month. At first, I told them how much I hated being in a big school and having passing time for classes. I longed for the familiar faces at my old school and the rooms I'd come to know and love. Mom kept telling me that getting used to something new can be hard at first, but things would get better. It didn't take long to realize that telling them about my problems only made things worse. Because then they felt the need to ask about every little thing, and I just didn't want to talk to them about it.

Instead, I write haiku. Strange, I know, but it helps. My fifth-grade teacher, Ms. Lennon, got me started. She shared one almost every day on the whiteboard last year. I kind of became obsessed and started coming up with my own. My brain loves counting syllables, apparently. And when something good comes to me, I try to write it down.

Since I'd been eating lunch in the library, I liked to write them on little pieces of paper and slip them into books for others to find. Like this one I'd written earlier today:

Three years of this, but others have survived and so will I. Hopefully.

For a moment, I thought about reciting it as my answer to her question. But instead, I turned to my mom, smiled, and replied, "Fine."

"Learn anything interesting?" Dad asked.

I knew they didn't like it when I answered with just one word. But did they understand I didn't like it when they asked about school every single day? Because honestly, they might have *thought* they'd love to know what it's like for me in middle school, but did they really?

I mean, did they *really* want to know there were a couple of boys who insisted on tripping my best friend, Tori, and me every day as we made our way to first period? Did they *really* want to know I'd asked for permission to eat in the library because kids in the cafeteria were so obnoxious, sometimes I could hardly stand it? Did they *really* want to know that in band class, I kept finding a note on my music stand with some horrible comment about my butt?

As much as I didn't want to show them, I knew I had to, and this was my chance. I pulled the piece of paper out of the pocket of my jeans, unfolded it, and placed it in the middle of our table for them to read.

"Yeah, this happened today," I whispered. "And, Mom, please, keep your voice down, okay?"

And then I held my breath, hoping she'd grant me my wish.

CHAPTER TWO

"Oh no," Mom said after she read it. "No, no, no. This can't be real. Not here. Not in our nice little town."

That nice little town is Willow, Oregon, although it seems pretty big to me. Dad often talks about our city's "growing pains" and how things have changed a lot in the past ten years. He thinks people are moving away from the expensive cities, hoping for a quieter life while still having the beach close by in one direction and the mountains nearby in the other. Oregon is a beautiful place, for sure. I couldn't help but wonder if maybe this piece of paper was another one of Willow's growing pains.

And sadly, the dress code they were looking at *was* real. Since I'd started middle school, I'd watched our principal, Mr. Buck, scold quite a few girls before school because of their wardrobe choices. And then, what do you know, the school board had met Wednesday night and voted on it, and now our entire school district had a brand-new policy in place.

"Mom, it doesn't even affect me that much," I said. "You know I don't wear shorts or tank tops. That's not me. So please, just sign it and I'll take it back Monday."

"But, honey, it doesn't matter that it doesn't affect you. It's the message that it sends—that girls' bodies are dangerous, so we better cover them up. That the girls are responsible for any problems because of what they wear, not the boys. Do you see what I mean?"

I nodded. "Yeah. I guess I didn't really think about it like that."

Dad piped in. "Me either, I'm sorry to say, and I'm a guy who's been around a while."

Mom continued, "Plus, the way I read this is that if a bra strap accidentally peeks out from your shirt, you could be written up or sent home to change. I mean, listen to this line; it's really troublesome: 'In all cases, the administration will decide whether or not students are adhering to the dress code standards.'"

Mom shook her head and was about to say more when the return of my burger saved me. All hail the life-saving hamburger!

"Here you are," the waiter said. "Again, my apologies."

"It's okay," I told him.

After he left, I cut it in half with a knife this time so I could see what it looked like before biting into it.

"Looks good!" Dad said. "And they even gave you more fries for your troubles. You should never feel bad about speaking up, Hazel. Nothing good comes from keeping quiet if you're unhappy."

9

Obviously, my dad is a lot more optimistic than I am, because all I could think about as I took a bite of my burger was, *I hope the cook didn't spit on it to get back at me for asking for a second one.*

Maybe optimism is another superpower people get when they're older. Probably after they're out of school. I bet it's a lot easier to be optimistic about everything in life when there's no school to worry about.

Mom seemed to still be dissecting the dress code policy. "They say this is about creating a safe and positive learning environment, but what it does is shame students. Mostly girls. It's not right." She pushed the paper back toward me. "I'm going to call and speak to Mr. Buck on Monday. If a number of parents call, maybe we can get it changed."

I'd gotten a text from Tori earlier, letting me know her moms were pretty upset as well. Maybe my mom was right. Maybe if enough parents complained, they'd reverse the policy. It affected Tori more than me, since she liked to wear tank tops sometimes.

"So, you're not going to sign it?" I asked. Both of us were supposed to sign it and return it to the school. "Signing it doesn't mean you approve of it; they just want to know that you've read it."

"No," she said firmly. "I won't do it. Not yet. Let me see what he says on Monday."

"You want me to call him?" Dad asked. "I'm happy to do it."

"Hmm. That's not a bad idea," Mom said. "He might be more willing to listen to another man, unfortunately." She shook her head. "But let me think about it."

We finished eating, mostly in silence, which was fine with me. Dad paid the check and then we left. It felt like a dark cloud hung over us as we made our way to the car. I didn't like it. But then something happened that turned things right around. I noticed a cardboard box sitting on a yellow parking bumper in the parking lot, like someone had parked, pulled it out of the car, and set it there. I ran over to see what was inside.

"What is it, Hazel?" Dad asked.

"You won't believe it," I said. I knelt down and gently touched it.

Mom and Dad both came over and peered inside.

"What in the world?" Mom asked. "Who would leave a turtle in the parking lot?"

"Someone who didn't want their pet tortoise anymore," Dad said. "How terribly sad."

The tortoise was about the size of a soccer ball. A flat soccer ball, obviously. Its shell was really beautiful, with tan and brown markings. It kind of looked like the shell was covered in large, knobby scales, with a light brown spot in the middle of each one. It had black eyes, and there were red spots on its head and feet. I was a little nervous about picking it up, even though I wanted to. I figured there would be time for that later. So I tucked my book underneath my arm and picked up the cardboard box.

"What are you doing, Hazel?" Mom asked.

"I can't just leave it here," I said. "It's abandoned and alone. If it were a puppy or a kitten, you'd insist on taking it home, wouldn't you? We should do the right thing."

Mom looked around. "What if its owner comes back? What if it was a mistake?"

"I don't think it's a mistake," Dad said. "Sadly, people abandon pets all the time because they can't care for them anymore." He looked at me. "Do you know anything about tortoises, Hazel?"

"No, do you?" I asked.

Both of them shook their heads.

We'd had an old tabby cat named Felix that had been my mom's since just after college. He died last year and Mom was so sad, she said she didn't want another one for a while.

But a tortoise was very different from a cat. Maybe I'd just found the perfect new pet for our family.

CHAPTER THREE

My parents agreed to stop at Tori's house on the way home so I could show her what I'd found. I thought about texting Tori to let her know, but I wanted to surprise her. One of Tori's moms, Jeanie, works as a veterinary technician, so it seemed like she might have some advice on how to take care of the tortoise.

By the time we got to their cute blue house, it was dark, but Tori and her two moms were sitting in comfy chairs on the large front porch that has string lights hung all around it. I didn't see Tori's older brother, Ben, around, although that seemed to be the way it was lately. Tori and her moms often sit on the cozy porch after dinner, listening to an audiobook. Tori has dyslexia, so listening to books is easier for her than reading them.

"Love that they still have the banner up," Dad said, pointing to where it hung between two trees along the side of their property. It read, WE LOVE OUR WILLOW LITTLE LEAGUE TEAM!

Ben's baseball team went all the way to the Little League championship game last summer during the World Series. They lost, but the whole city of Willow was behind them and while Ben was popular before, as the star pitcher, I think it catapulted him to a new level.

He used to like doing things with Tori and me. At least, I thought he did. We used to play restaurant in the mornings when I slept over. We'd make him a menu and then he'd choose what he wanted us to cook and pretend to be our customer. Okay, so maybe that was more about getting fed than hanging out with us, but there were other things, too. For years, he loved coming to cheer at our soccer games. In between games, we'd kick the soccer ball around in their yard and he'd give us pointers. We'd tease him and call him coach and then he'd yell at us (in a funny sort of way) and make us do push-ups and sit-ups.

Four months ago or so, all of it just . . . stopped. I noticed whenever I went to their house, he was mostly in his room with the door shut. A few weeks ago, I was with Tori when she knocked on Ben's door and asked, "What are you doing?" All she got was, "None of your business."

I think one of the worst feelings in the world is when someone stops liking you for no good reason. It's like flunking a test and never getting it back to see what answers you got wrong. Why? What happened? What'd I do?

I couldn't imagine not wanting to sit on that porch on a warm fall night with some of the best people I'd ever known. But I also wasn't a thirteen-year-old boy. Who even knows what goes on in their brains.

The three of them waved as we all got out of the car.

Alice, who Tori calls Mimi, reached over and turned off the CD player. "Hello, Wallace Family," she said. "What a nice surprise."

"Wait until you see what I brought to show you," I said.

Tori hopped down the steps and ran toward our car while my parents made their way up to the porch to talk to Tori's moms. "What? What'd you bring?"

I opened the door to the back seat, the dome light spilling out around us, and carefully moved the box to Tori's yard. "We found it in the parking lot of Ruby's. We think someone just didn't want it anymore. Isn't that sad?"

"Wow," Tori said, her eyes big and round. "If I'd have guessed a hundred times, I never would have guessed that this is what you wanted to show us." She didn't seem at all nervous as she reached into the box and gently picked up the tortoise. "Can I show my moms?"

"Yes, please," I said. "I'm curious if Jeanie will know what kind it is and what I should feed it."

She carried the tortoise carefully with both hands as she went back toward the house. I followed close behind. "Why, that's a red-footed tortoise," Jeanie said when Tori handed it to her. "A very popular type for pets because they're an easy size to handle. People also love how they look. Isn't he a beauty?"

"What's the difference between a turtle and a tortoise?" Tori asked.

Jeanie responded, "Well, a tortoise is a type of turtle. True turtles mostly live in water, while tortoises live on land."

"I've always wanted to swim with the sea turtles in Hawaii," my mom said.

"Oh yes, me too," Alice said. "They're magnificent creatures, aren't they?"

"Maybe we should plan a trip to Maui together," Dad said. "I haven't been in years, and I bet the kids would love it."

While the four of them discussed everything they loved about the Hawaiian Islands, Tori and I were still focused on the magnificent creature right in front of us.

"Why would someone just leave him like that, Mom?" Tori asked.

"Hard to say," Jeanie said. "Happens a lot, unfortunately, with all kinds of pets. Sometimes people have to move, and they can't take their pet with them. Sometimes they're dealing with a health issue or a job loss and don't have the finances anymore. Would you like me to make an appointment for the vet to take a look at him on Monday? Make sure he's in good health?"

"Oh, thank you, that'd be wonderful," Mom said. "Afternoon would be best for me."

"Sure, I'll text you and let you know what time we can see him," Jeanie said.

"I love its little feet," Tori said as she reached over and touched one of them. "Wait, Mom, you said 'him.' Does that mean you know for sure that it's a boy?"

"Yes, it does," Jeanie said as she handed the tortoise to me. Now that I'd seen both of them hold him, I wasn't so nervous about it. I placed one hand underneath him and the other hand on top of his pretty shell, which felt smooth and hard. I held on tightly, since the last thing I wanted to do was drop him.

Jeanie explained. "See his tail? Females have short, stubby tails, while the males' are quite a bit longer. As soon as I saw the tail, I knew it was a male."

"I guess the name I was thinking of won't work, then," I replied. "I thought Pippi would be perfect."

"What about Pip?" Tori asked. "Short and sweet."

I smiled. "Hey, I love that!"

I held him up high so I could get a good look at his face. "How's that sound, buddy? Do you like the name Pip?" His beady little eyes stared at me and the name seemed good and right and true. He was so unique. I'd never held anything like him.

Tori leaned in and whispered in my ear, "Are you going to keep him?"

In that moment, it felt like I'd never wanted anything more. The first line of a haiku popped into my head and from there, the rest fell right into place. I love it when one comes so easily like that.

Sweet little tortoise,
looking for someone to love.
My heart says, yes please!

We chatted for a few more minutes, mostly about caring for him, and just as Mom said it was time for us to head home, Jeanie added, "You should probably keep in mind that tortoises can live for eighty years or longer."

I gulped. "Eighty years?"

Jeanie nodded. "Pretty extraordinary, isn't it? This one doesn't look very old, either, though we'll know more once the vet looks him over."

"Maybe the school library has some books on tortoises," Tori suggested as she walked me down the steps. "So you can learn everything about them to help you decide whether you should keep him or not."

"Good idea," I said. My parents were ahead of us, still talking with Tori's moms. I whispered to Tori, "Sounds like Mr. Buck is going to get an earful on Monday. Your moms aren't the only ones who are furious."

"I tried to tell them it's not that big of a deal," she whispered back, "but I have a feeling they'll be showing up at the next school board meeting. I just hope they don't make me look bad somehow. We're still trying to prove ourselves, you know? I don't want them to ruin our chances of becoming popular."

Becoming popular was something Tori wanted really

badly. She talked about it a lot. Worried about it, even. But me? This was middle school and honestly, from what I'd seen so far, all I wanted to do was survive.

"At least we have parents who care about us and want to make sure we're treated fairly, right?" I said.

"Yeah. You're right. See you tomorrow morning!" Tori said as I got in the car. "I have a good feeling about this one!"

I laughed. "You say that about every game."

"Well, I've been right this whole season, haven't I?"

Our team was undefeated so far this year. It was pretty exciting.

"You gonna wear your lucky socks?" I asked as Dad started the car.

"Yes!" she said. "And because they've been so lucky, I'm not even washing them. I don't want to break the streak."

We all laughed as we drove away. Hopefully the popular kids wouldn't get a whiff of Tori's sock situation. Like, literally.

CHAPTER FOUR

Tori and I started playing soccer together in third grade. Every year that I've played, I've fallen in love with the game a little more. But Tori, not so much. She seemed to be getting more and more frustrated by it. She wasn't as good as she wished she could be. She's pretty quick on the field, but she's not very skilled at dribbling and passing the ball.

"You're so much stronger than I am," she told me once. "Like, your legs are pure muscle."

"You mean big?" I said.

"No," she said. "No! That's not what I meant, I swear."

Tori's about the same height as I am, but our bodies are not similar at all. She's like a graceful gazelle while I'm a stocky rhino. Mom has always told me that I shouldn't compare myself to other girls. She says that everyone is shaped differently and there is no right or wrong body shape. I know she's right, but it's still hard sometimes.

I remember the first time I started worrying about how I looked. It was in third grade when I'd worn shorts to field day on the last day of school. A boy named Dustin had called me Thunder Thighs, and I'd come home crying. My parents said they didn't understand "how a child would even know that term." But it didn't matter. Dustin knew that nickname and then I knew it and it was all I thought of for a long time when I looked at my legs.

"Am I fat?" I'd asked Mom. "Am I fat and you just haven't told me? Do I need to go on a diet?"

My mom had looked like she wanted to cry. "No," she'd said, her voice shaking. "There will be no diets in this house. There is nothing wrong with your body, Hazel. Not a single thing. It houses that wonderful brain and heart of yours. It gets you around this world. And it helps you to be one of the best soccer players on your team! I'm so thankful for that amazing body of yours, and you should be, too."

I wanted to see it the way my mom saw it. But it's hard. Since then, I've only worn shorts to play soccer. Not Tori, though. She loves shorts and would probably wear them every day if she could, even when it's thirty-two degrees out and snowing.

"My legs feel like they're suffocating when I have to wear pants," she told me one time. "They need to breathe. I have to get them off as soon as I get home or I feel like I'm going to die."

"Oh no, gonna die from wearing pants, HALLLLP," I'd teased. But it was true. She hated pants and that was that. Since we had a dress code at school now that specifically mentioned shorts, I wondered if she might decide to wear long skirts more often. As for me, I'd stick to jeans, thank you very much.

When I got out of bed on Saturday, I said good morning to Pip, who'd slept in his box in my room, and then I put on my blue-and-white uniform. I'd chosen 20 for my jersey because it was Abby Wambach's number when she played on the US Women's Team. I have such happy memories of watching her on TV when she played in both the World Cup and the Olympics. She's probably the biggest reason I wanted to play soccer. And not just play but work hard at it so maybe some-day I can play professionally, too. Having her number on my jersey reminds me of that goal every time I put it on.

My cleats were in my duffel bag along with an extra pair of shorts, a towel, and my water bottle, which I needed to refill. I carried everything downstairs and went into the kitchen. Mom was there, drinking coffee and staring out the window.

"Hi, Mom," I said as I took my water bottle to the sink.

"Good morning," she said.

"What can I give Pip to eat?"

"There's half a bag of kale in the refrigerator. Give him some of that for now. I'll go to the store later and get some other things. Make sure he has fresh water. Oh, and I think you should put his box near the window, so he gets some sunshine."

"Okay." I put my full water bottle into my bag and grabbed the kale out of the fridge. "Be right back."

"Want me to make you some eggs?"

"No, thanks. Just feel like Cheerios today."

I quickly got Pip situated so he'd be okay by himself and then ran back to the kitchen for some breakfast.

After I sat down at the table with my cereal, a banana, and a glass of orange juice, I sent a photo to Tori and a few other girls from our team with the caption: BREAKFAST OF CHAMPIONS!

For a long time, Mom and Dad had said I couldn't have a phone until I was thirteen. Last summer, they changed their minds and Mom gave me her old phone when she upgraded. But there were some rules, of course. It had to be turned off and put away at school. The camera was not to be used for selfies. And I couldn't get any social media accounts until high school.

"The selfie culture is not a good thing for girls your age," Mom had told me. "Actually, it's probably not a good thing for girls at any age, but I think it's especially harmful for young girls."

"I don't know what you mean," I'd said.

"Hazel, the constant comparison that happens on social media is very unhealthy. I know it may be hard for you to believe right now, but how we look is at the bottom of the list of things that are important in life. Selfies make it feel like it's at the top of the list. That you are a nothing and a nobody if you aren't getting a thousand likes with every picture of yourself. It's absurd when you think about it because what matters, what *truly* matters, is how you treat others and figuring out how you can make a difference in this world for the better."

I swear she sounded like an advertisement—just say no to selfies! It was a lot to think about and she was probably right about most of it. Still, I was super disappointed. A *lot* of girls at school already had socials. I tried to tell myself that I was lucky to have a phone at all, but it was hard sometimes.

After I finished my breakfast, Dad came down and we all got in the car to go to the game.

"Got a new playlist for you this morning," Dad said.

Dad loved making game-day playlists for me. He'd put songs on it like "All I Do Is Win" and "Let's Get It Started."

"Listen to this song," he said as he turned up the volume. "It's called 'Here Comes the Boom' and I think it'll really get you pumped."

Mom and I laughed. But still, how cute was it that my dad was trying so hard to get me "pumped" for my games?

When we got to the field, my closest friends on the team besides Tori, Abigail, and Sasha, greeted me with high fives and we started kicking a ball around to warm up. It was a gray, misty day. I love that kind of weather. Soccer-playing weather, for sure. The soft, green grass felt good under my cleats as I passed the ball back to Abigail.

"Hey, better watch out. Your bra strap is peeking out of your jersey," Sasha teased Abigail.

Abigail quipped back, "Sure thing, Mr. Buck, let me take care of that right now. Because oh, those poor, poor boys just can't handle a normal piece of clothing, right?"

She whipped her jersey off and stood there in her black sports bra. And even though there was nothing offensive or indecent about it, because it just looked like a short tank top, it was kind of shocking to see it happen. But everyone on the team started cheering.

And then, much to my surprise, Sasha took off her jersey, too. And then Tori. And then another girl did it. And another. Before long, half the team stood on the field in just their sports bras.

I couldn't do it. No way. They were all so much braver than I was. But I did wish Mr. Buck could have been there to see that there's no evil in bras.

Eventually, they had to put their jerseys on so we could start the game. And what a game it was. We won six to two, and I scored two goals. There is nothing like the feeling of scoring. Nothing. In that moment, when I see the ball go in, it's like the world is made of chocolate and rainbows and unicorns.

After we'd shaken hands with the other team, I ran toward my parents, who were sitting with Jeanie and Alice. Tori followed close behind me.

We got our hugs and congratulations and then Jeanie

said, "Hazel, I asked your parents if you could go to the zoo with us today and they said yes. That is, if you want to. These clouds are supposed to clear off soon and it should be a nice fall day."

Tori beamed. "One thing about Hazel? She'll never say no to elephants, right?"

"For sure," I agreed.

I love elephants so much. My dream is to visit one of the elephant sanctuaries in Thailand one day. Although I'm worried that when my dream finally comes true, I'll just want to move in and live with them. I don't know what it is about them, exactly, but I think they're incredible.

I actually cried when one of the Oregon Zoo's elephants passed away last year. Lily was only six years old when a deadly virus hit her, and there wasn't anything they could do for her. I was heartbroken about it for at least a week.

"We want to get going," Alice said, "so is it okay if we take you home with us and you wear something of Tori's today?"

This worried me a little bit. What if I couldn't fit into any of Tori's clothes? I had some shorts I could wear, despite my dislike of them, but I'd need to borrow a shirt.

"Sure," I said, trying to sound enthusiastic.

It was almost like Tori could read my mind. "Don't worry. We'll find you something good to wear."

Mom reached into her purse and took out her wallet. She handed me a twenty-dollar bill and then my phone, which she always keeps for me while I play. "Make sure to grab your bag. Your shoes are in there so you won't have to wear your cleats all day. Will you text me and let me know when you get there? And please, stay alert. Be safe."

"I know, Mom." I said goodbye to my parents and then ran off behind Tori to find Jeanie's truck.

We all piled in and as we headed toward their house, Tori asked Alice, "Mimi, can we make Ben go with us? He never does anything with us anymore."

"I'm not going to make him go," Alice responded. "But maybe if you two ask him nicely, he'll decide he'd like to come with us."

That seemed about as unlikely as Abby Wambach showing up at one of our games. But I kept my thoughts to myself. Besides soccer, it's the one thing I'm pretty good at.

CHAPTER FIVE

When we got to Tori's house, the two of us raced off to her room, saying hello to all their pets as we went. They have three cats, two dogs, and a partridge in a pear tree. Okay, not the last one, but they do have a big fish tank with lots of beautiful fish. When she told me she'd decided to call them all Shawn, I'd asked, "After Shawn Mendes, your crush to end all crushes?"

"No."

"Then why Shawn?"

"Because it works no matter what gender they are."

My best friend is very clever.

One of their cats, a gray one named Archie, lay on her bed. Maybe a turtle wasn't as soft and cuddly as a cat, but there wouldn't be any claws to worry about. I lay on my stomach and petted him while Tori opened her dresser drawers and then her closet doors. "Pick out whatever you want."

I chose an adorable tee that says TEA & BOOKS & CATS & NAPS. My brain wanted to write a haiku about those things, but I told it to wait because I was in a hurry and it's hard to do haiku while doing other things.

"I'll just wear my own shorts," I told her.

I started to take my shirt off and then decided maybe I should wash off in the bathroom first. "I'll be right back. I'm gonna get a wash cloth and . . ." I dabbed under one of my arm pits. "You know. Don't want to smell worse than the zoo animals."

She laughed. "But you'd fit right in!"

I grabbed my shorts and her shirt and as I dashed into the hallway, I ran into Ben. "Oh, sorry," I told him.

He smiled, looking like the old Ben I used to know. "Hey, no problem. Haven't seen you in a while. How's it going?"

Before I could answer, Tori came out to the hallway and said, "Ben, we're going to the zoo. Will you please go with us? *Please?* We'll have fun, I promise."

"Can't, Sis," he said. "Going to a friend's house. Have to study for a test."

Tori crossed her arms. "I don't believe you. We're just not cool enough for you, are we? All you care about anymore are your friends."

He laughed. "Tori, what are you talking about?"

"It's true!" she insisted. "You're not the studious type. I mean, since when does one of the most popular guys at school care about his grades?"

I don't know why it took until right then, but suddenly, I got it. Like, I *really* got it. For a while I'd wondered why Tori was so obsessed about becoming popular in middle school. Her intense questioning started last summer, when she'd ask Ben things like, "Where do the popular kids sit at lunch?" and "Can sixth graders sit with the seventh and eighth graders at assemblies, or are there separate sections for each grade?"

She was jealous. Jealous of her older brother who had lots of friends and girls chasing after him because he was so good-looking with his brown wavy locks and gorgeous green eyes. Tori wanted to be popular like Ben, and since the end of fifth grade, she'd been trying to figure out how to make it happen.

"So, I'm just gonna . . ." I pointed to the bathroom.

Still talking, they moved out of the way so I could get into the bathroom. I shut the door and locked it, wondering if I'd feel less awkward about getting in the middle of their fights if I had an older brother or sister. Sometimes being an only child makes me feel like an alien.

After I took off my shirt, I found a washcloth in the cupboard. Before I turned on the faucet, I heard Tori scream at her brother, "You're so selfish, Ben! All you think about is yourself." And then she slammed her bedroom door shut.

I'd washed the right armpit with soap and water and was about to do the left when there was a knock on the door.

"Hazel," Ben said. "Sorry to bother you, but I forgot my notebook in there. Can you hand it to me, please?"

"Just a sec," I called out.

"It's probably sitting on the back of the toilet."

"Okay, hold on, I need to get dressed."

I glanced over and sure enough, there was a small spiral notebook with a red cover. On the front, in big black letters, it said PRIVATE PROPERTY OF BEN R.

I don't know what made me do it. Maybe I felt like it would help me understand him better? Like, maybe there was a clue as to why he basically shut us out all of a sudden. Or maybe I'm just a terrible person who can't respect other people's property. Except I totally can. There was just something about that little notebook with such a strong message to keep out, I couldn't help but look.

I opened it and on the inside of the front cover, someone had written, "Cute or nah? Rate them, then date them, if you dare."

On the first lined page, there was a girl's name. Addie Sanders. And then rows of initials with numbers and comments below her name.

B.R. 9 SHE IS SO GORGEOUS, I DREAM ABOUT HER SOMETIMES
T.E. 10 doesn't get any better than this girl
J.J. 8 too tall for me
V.R. 5 uh, have you seen her teeth? The girl needs braces so bad
P.W. 9 such a babe. Who looks at her teeth anyway?

I could hardly believe what I was reading. I closed the toilet lid and sat down before I carefully and quietly flipped the pages.

Each page was the same. A girl's name at the top and then ratings and comments below. Many of the names I didn't recognize, but some I did. Like, I'm in a study hall that has sixth through eighth graders and I saw a few names from girls in that class, all in different grades. I also saw names of some of my friends who play soccer with me.

And then, I had a thought that made my stomach hurt so much, I was afraid I might throw up.

Would I find my name in here?

I started to flip the pages, looking, when something made me stop.

TORI ROBINSON
DON'T EVEN THINK ABOUT IT.

So Tori was saved. But what about me?

Ben knocked again, startling me so much, I dropped the notebook. "Hazel, come on. Just crack the door and give it to me."

I threw on the shirt and opened the door. "Sorry," I said as he snatched it from my hand.

He waved it in the air. "Thanks. I need it to study for that test, you know?" He sounded normal. But he wore a smug half-smile that screamed, "I'm so amazing; I can get away with anything."

I didn't know what to say, so I just mumbled, "Okay."

He turned and rambled down the hallway. "See you later. Have fun at the zoo!"

I shut the door again and tried to slow my breathing as I began to process what had just happened. Ben had a notebook filled with girls' names and was passing it around, getting guys to rate them. And I had no idea if I was in there and what they might be saying about me.

Why had I rushed to give it to him before I knew? I was pretty sure I'd never be able to sleep until I got an answer.

CHAPTER SIX

I coaxed Tori out of her room and into Alice's car. We listened to an audiobook as we drove the hour and a half up to Portland. It was a historical novel called *Under a Painted Sky*, about two girls who dressed up as boys to stay safe as they made their way on the Oregon Trail. They were headed for the California gold rush all on their own. Alice said the book is fiction, but the story was so good, it seemed real. I couldn't help but think how messed up it was that two girls had to dress as boys to stay as safe as possible, though.

As good as the book was, my mind wandered to what I'd found in the bathroom. I was thankful I didn't have to talk to anyone during the ride because I'm not sure I would have been able to keep my thoughts to myself. Except I knew I couldn't tell Tori or her moms. If they knew about the list of girls, they would be so upset. Like, really, really upset.

I mean, it made me upset and I wasn't even related to Ben.

But even if I decided to tell them (which seemed impossible, honestly), would they believe me? And would they be angry that I'd snooped? The cover of the notebook said

PRIVATE in big, black letters. There wasn't a single good reason why I should have opened it. Not one.

When we made it to the zoo, I texted my mom and let her know. She replied:

Grandma and Grandpa are coming for dinner tonight. The zoo closes at four in the fall, so you'll be home in plenty of time. Have fun!

This was good news! Grandma loved animals, and I couldn't wait to introduce her to Pip. My parents and I hadn't talked about whether or not we would keep Pip, but I knew that conversation was coming.

The first thing the four of us did after we'd bought our admission tickets was to get some food since it was after noon and we were starving. While we ate our lunch, we talked about our favorite animals at the zoo so we could make sure not to miss visiting them all.

"You already know mine," I said.

"Fuzzy lemurs for me," Tori said.

"Giraffes," Alice said.

"Naked mole rats," Jeanie said.

"Ew," Alice said, turning to Jeanie with her face all scrunched up. "That's even worse than saying the bats."

"Oh, I love the bats too," she said. "So creepy yet beautiful."

Tori shivered. "Mom, you're weird. Bats are so gross."

"Honey, it's not nice to put someone down for simply liking something," Jeanie said. "Please remember that, okay?"

I could tell by the look on Tori's face that she felt bad. "Okay. Sorry."

I kind of wanted to say, "What about boys who like rating girls? It's okay to put them down, right?" But I kept quiet. I needed to just forget about what I'd seen. There wasn't anything I could do about it, anyway. I kept telling myself that maybe Ben had protected me the way he'd protected Tori. I wanted to believe there wasn't a page about me in the book.

Tori put her arm around my shoulders. "I'm definitely not going to put Hazel down for loving the elephants because they are pretty incredible, but naked mole rats? Why? They're so creepy looking."

"They dig underground with their teeth," Jeanie explained. "They hardly ever use their eyes, but their hearing is incredible. I just think they're really unusual."

"So, how do we decide what we see first?" I asked.

"The elephants are out with the trainers," Tori said, pointing toward the fairly new outdoor habitat that we could see from our outside table. "I say let's check them out right now."

A few months ago, I watched a video titled "Life after Lily." It talked about how the elephants at the zoo were starting to come around after losing her. Back to their normal selves. A few of the keepers in the video talked about how difficult Lily's death had been for them. That she had been a little ray of sunshine for them every day. Since her passing, they'd been giving her mom, Rose, extra attention and treats. It was one of the saddest videos I'd ever seen. It had shown me that the keepers considered the elephants their family.

Each of the zookeepers now stood next to an elephant. Some of them were brushing their elephants. Some were picking up their feet and checking them. And one held a bucket with some kind of food and threw it to an elephant swimming in the pool. The elephant looked so happy, lounging in the water, its trunk raised, opening its mouth to catch the snack every time the zookeeper tossed food.

To be honest, zoos are something I have mixed feelings about. If I had my way, all elephants could live happily in the wild. But maybe when people come to the zoo and see the animals, they'll realize how special they are and be willing to take better care of our planet, for us and for them. Maybe?

"I've always wanted to play with the elephants," I told Tori. "But maybe what I really want is to *be* an elephant."

"Don't you want to be something cuter?" she asked. "A lemur, maybe? Some kind of bear? Or what about an otter? I love otters."

"But Tori, looks aren't everything. Or they shouldn't be, right?"

She raised her eyebrows. "You're a bit spicy today."

"Spicy?"

She nodded her head toward Alice. "Something Mimi likes to say."

I wiggled my eyebrows. "Pretty sure it's your spiciness that's rubbed off on me. But think about it. Their trunks are so amazing. They're smart. And very family-oriented. And better than cute, they're, like, majestic. That's the best word to describe them, I think. Majestic."

"Okay, okay, I get it," Tori said. "You adore elephants, and nothing will change that fact."

But now I was back to thinking about the list of girls and how all the boys had decided nothing else mattered.

Not how kind they were.

Not how smart they were.

Not whether they were funny or artistic or athletic.

It seemed the only thing that mattered to most of the boys at our school was looks. I thought of other things in the world that were viewed differently than girls, and my brain couldn't help but count syllables.

Trees lose their pretty
leaves in autumn, but no one
shames them for that fact.

Beautiful. Pretty. Cute. Gorgeous. Babe. How many times had my parents and grandparents said, "You're so cute!" when I was younger? How many times have I wondered why I hardly ever heard that as I've gotten older?

My hair's too frizzy. My nose too crooked. My lips too big.

Every day I think at least one of these things and beat myself up for it. Last year when I got a cold sore on my bottom lip and it grew three sizes bigger, I asked my mom if I could stay home from school.

"Honey, you need to go to school," Mom said. "The kids will understand." But she was wrong. They didn't understand at all.

This mean kid, Thomas, told everyone at recess, "Look at Hazel, she has camel lips!"

Some of the kids thought it was hilarious, and for weeks, boys called me Camel Lips. It only stopped because one of the teachers heard it once and told them if it happened again, she'd write them up and call their parents.

Did someone remember that and write it under my name in that notebook? Or did they talk about my thunder thighs? Or maybe how I had wildly thick hair that was harder to tame than a mustang?

I was terrified to know but also *dying* to know.

How could I possibly make it the next three years knowing a notebook was being passed around school where boys could say horrible things about me?

"Are you okay?" Tori asked.

I wasn't okay. Not at all. And the really awful thing was I had no idea what to do about it.

CHAPTER SEVEN

On the way home, we listened to music instead of the book. Tori flipped through a fashion magazine, pointing things out to me.

"I'm glad that frilly sleeves seem to be going out of style," she said. "Remember when I tried on that blouse with big ruffles up and down the arms that made me look like a clown?"

Almost every time Tori and Alice go shopping, she invites me to go, too. I don't like shopping half as much as Tori, but since I do need to buy clothes now and then, sometimes I tag along.

"Since T-shirts are basically the same now as they've always been, I don't think I need to worry about going out of style anytime soon," I teased.

"But aren't you worried about looking as good as everyone else?"

"Tori, that's not very nice," Alice said, looking at us in the rearview mirror. "It sounds like you're insulting her."

Tori put her hands in the air. "I didn't mean it like that, I swear. I just meant . . . it matters what we wear now, more than it did in elementary school. Even Ben told us that last year, when he was giving us tips about middle school. You remember that, right, Hazel?"

I did remember it. That conversation was probably the last good one we'd had with Ben. We'd gone out for ice cream to celebrate moving on from Hoover Elementary and Ben had given us a bunch of advice.

"Try not to stand out," he'd told us. "You want to look good, not like some messy, immature elementary kids. Clothes are definitely more important in middle school. But you shouldn't look *too* good, you know? If you stand out, you'll be a target."

"A target for what?" I'd asked.

"All kinds of things, I guess. I mean, who knows? But that's my point—don't stand out and you probably won't have to worry about it."

"You're not making any sense, Ben," Tori had told him. "If I want to be popular, shouldn't I try to look as good as I possibly can?"

He shook his head. "If you try looking like a tenth grader when you're in sixth grade? That is not a wise move, Sis. You gotta trust me on that."

"I'm just gonna be my normal, boring self, so I'm sure it'll be fine," I told them.

He seemed completely serious when he said, "If you girls ever have any trouble, feel free to come to me, okay?"

Now I had some trouble with a certain notebook, but going to Ben seemed about as impossible as flying to Mars.

"You obviously take after your mimi, Tori," Jeanie said. "I've always been more like Hazel. Being comfortable is about my only requirement when it comes to clothes. When I met your mimi in college, I wasn't sure if she'd even want to go out with me since we were so different that way. You know how much she loves fashion." She reached over and held Alice's hand. "Fortunately, she didn't hold my lack of style against me."

Alice smiled at her wife. "I mean, just because I love a well put-together outfit doesn't mean I expect everyone to be that way. You knew how to win me over."

"How?" Tori asked.

Jeanie laughed. "I asked her if she wanted to go out for the best mac and cheese she'd ever have in her life."

Now Alice chuckled. "And I couldn't say yes fast enough!"

"Mmm, now I want some good mac and cheese," Tori said.

"Same!" I declared.

"I know what I'm making for dinner tonight!" Alice said. "Want to join us, Hazel? You're more than welcome."

"Thanks, but my grandparents are coming over," I told them.

"Lucky you," Jeanie said. "I'd take my grandparents over mac and cheese any day of the week."

Tori didn't seem to know what to say to that, since her great-grandparents on Jeanie's side had been gone for a while now, and I know they all missed them. She opened her magazine again and pointed to a jumpsuit. "This would look so cute on you."

"Cuter on you," I told her.

Which was probably true about everything, but I didn't say that.

When we got to my house, I grabbed my bag and hopped out of the car, calling, "Thank you, that was fun!"

We waved goodbye and then I ran inside.

Everyone was in the kitchen either helping with the meal or setting the table. It smelled like basil and oregano and all the other yummy things Mom puts in her lasagna sauce.

"There's our girl," Grandma said as she pulled me close for a hug. "Decided to come home instead of joining the elephants, huh?"

"Let me guess," Grandpa said. "You smuggled one home in your bag."

"I wish," I said.

Grandpa winked. "I guess I know what to get you for Christmas."

Grandma and Grandpa are the cutest couple I've ever seen. They both have silver hair, they both wear bifocals, *and* they both love to dance. They're not that old, sixty-two, and it's one of their favorite things to do together. We all went to a wedding once, and when my grandparents got on the dance floor and started doing their swing danc-ing, everyone clapped and cheered. Sometimes when they're at our house, I'll put on some music and beg them to dance. And they always do. They don't get embarrassed or anything.

"Did either of you show them Pip?" I asked Mom and Dad.

"No, we thought we'd let you do that," Mom said.

"Pip?" Grandpa asked. "What's a Pip?"

"Don't tell!" I called to my parents as I ran up the stairs. "Let's surprise them."

I cleaned out Pip's box, since he'd made some messes, then carried him downstairs. Grandma and Grandpa both came over to take a look.

"Well, look at that," Grandpa said. "You got yourself a tortoise."

Mom explained how we'd found him while I got some more kale from the fridge.

"Are you going to keep him, then?" Grandma asked.

"We haven't actually talked about that yet," Mom said. "There's a lot to consider given that they live so long."

"Why does that matter so much, anyway?" I asked.

Grandma came over and put her arm around my shoul-ders. "It's a very big commitment, sweetheart. And it'd probably be hard to have other pets with a tortoise around, unless you want to keep it in a box or tank all the time, which seems pretty sad to me."

"Yes," Dad said. "It would need to be your only pet for the rest of your life."

I stared at Pip. My heart was telling me it was fine, I should keep him, but my brain was saying a lot of other things. What happened when I went away to college? I was pretty sure dorms didn't allow pets of any kind. And someday, if I got married and had kids, what happened if my family wanted a different kind of pet, like a dog or a cat?

I looked up at Dad. "But if I don't keep him, what will happen to him?"

Mom knelt by the box. She reached in and stroked his shell. "We could see if the Oregon Reptile Man might want him. He travels around and does reptile shows."

I shook my head. Hard. "No. Pip would hardly get any attention if he lived with so many other animals. If I give him up, we have to find someone with a lot of love to give. He deserves to be loved. A whole, whole lot."

"You have a good heart, Hazel," Grandpa said.

I wasn't so sure about that. If I had a good heart, wouldn't I have said I wanted to keep him, no matter what?

CHAPTER EIGHT

Flowers bloom in spring.
They don't wonder, they just know.
That must be so nice.

After dinner, we played the game Apples to Apples. I couldn't stop yawning. Between winning our soccer game, finding a notebook filled with awful things, and taking a fun trip to the zoo, it'd been a long day. When it got to the point where I wasn't sure if I could keep my eyes open any longer, I wished everyone good night and carried Pip in his box upstairs with me.

I really liked that sweet turtle. But I also knew it was possible that someday my life could change so much I might not be able to care for him. I needed to do what was best for Pip, not me. He needed a place where he would be loved and taken care of forever and ever. The more we had talked about it over dinner, the more I'd realized we needed to find him a new home.

Where should I look? Who could I ask? I didn't have a clue. I wondered if Tori might have some ideas, so when

I woke up Sunday morning, I sent her a text and asked if she wanted to meet for cinnamon rolls at Ruby's. When she said yes, I hopped out of bed, threw on some clothes, brushed my teeth, and took care of Pip by cleaning out his box and getting him some new veggies to eat.

"Where are you headed?" Dad asked when I came downstairs dressed and ready to go.

"Tori and I are going to meet up at Ruby's," I said. "Sorry, I should have asked first."

Dad smiled. "It's okay. Need some money?"

"Yes, please."

After he handed me the cash, I kissed him on the cheek and ran to the garage to get my bike.

When I got to Ruby's, I parked my bike next to Tori's and went inside. It smelled delicious—like sweet, fluffy pancakes with a side of bacon.

My family and I had been coming to the diner for as long as I could remember. I'd heard other kids complain that they didn't like it because it wasn't one of the latest and greatest restaurant chains, but that was exactly why I liked it. It was the kind of place where two sixth graders could come by themselves and feel welcomed. Here, it felt like they treated everyone as family. I wished I could feel as comfortable in other places as I did here. Except when I had to send a hamburger back, obviously. Fortunately, there would be no hamburgers for breakfast.

Tori sat at a booth with two cups of hot cocoa in front of

her. As I slid in, she told me, "I went ahead and ordered for you. Cinnamon rolls will be here soon."

"Thanks," I said. Then I noticed the cotton shirt she had on. It was white with little bluebirds all over it. "I love your shirt. Is that new?"

She grabbed a piece of the fabric on the sleeve with two fingers. "Yeah, Mimi bought it for me on a whim from that new little store that just opened, Sweet Pea Boutique. I told her I want to go next time, since they supposedly have super cute stuff. As for this, I guess I can only wear it on the weekends now."

"How come?"

She pointed toward the back. "Has a crisscross back, so you can see my bra straps."

I groaned. "Because bra straps are the absolute worst thing happening in our world right now, huh?"

Tori rolled her eyes. "Don't you love how they sent that new policy home on a Friday? They're probably hoping everyone will forget about it by Monday. Not my moms, though. They're definitely calling the school office first thing Monday."

"Yeah, I'm pretty sure my mom put it on her calendar. Although my dad offered to call instead, which kind of surprised me."

Tori took a sip of her cocoa. "My moms say men can be feminists, too, and that it's important to have men standing up for women's rights."

"Yeah, I can see that."

"So how's Mr. Pip?" she asked.

I squeezed my folded hands on the table in front of me. "He's fine. And I really like him a lot. But I've decided . . . we've decided to look for a different home for him."

Her eyes grew big. "What? Why?"

"I'm not sure I only want one pet my entire life, you know? And if my mom and dad aren't all in, I couldn't ask them to watch him when I go to college or travel the world or whatever I end up doing."

She nodded. "I get it."

"So, you're not mad?"

"Mad? That you're going to find the poor homeless tortoise a good home? Of course not! Why did you think I'd be mad?"

"I don't know. I guess because I was so excited about him and that made you excited, too. Maybe mad wasn't the right word. Sad? Disappointed?"

She nodded. "We'll probably both be a little sad when we have to say goodbye. That's normal, right? So, how are you going to find him a good home, exactly? Because it seems like it may be a kind of hard thing to do."

"I don't know," I replied. "I thought you might have some ideas to help me. Mom said the Oregon Reptile Man might take him, but poor Pip would never get any attention that way. He deserves to be loved, you know?"

"Of course he does. What about the exotic rescue place

my mom talked about? They might be able to find him a home."

I scratched my chin. "Maybe. But if they have lots of other animals, some a lot more exotic and exciting than him, he could be ignored there, too. And that's the last thing I want."

Tori's eyes lit up. "What if we asked Mom to put up a sign at work? 'Free tortoise to good home.' Something like that?"

"Hey, good idea."

Our waitress came and set the plates with our warm, gooey cinnamon rolls in front of us. They smelled *so* good— like the best cinnamon-and-vanilla candle ever made, but better, obviously, because you can't eat a candle. I watched the white frosting drip down the sides of mine as we both thanked her.

"You girls need anything else?" Doreen asked. (I knew her name because she wore a name tag on her pink dress.)

"No, thank you," Tori and I said at the same time.

"It'll be okay," Tori said as she cut into her roll. "You'll find someone."

"I hope so."

Tori looked past me at the door as someone came in. "Oh, look, it's Maddie Gray, that gorgeous eighth grader." Tori raised her hand and waved, much more enthusiastically than I would have. I turned to see Maddie give the tiniest, hesitant wave back.

"Do you know her?" I asked.

"No, but I'd love to," Tori said. "She seems to have a lot of friends."

"Last week I heard boys whispering about her in the hallway, though," I replied. "Not very nice things. I guess because she looks more like an eighteen-year-old than a thirteen-year-old?"

"Oh, whatever," Tori said. "Most middle school boys are gross. I'm just going to ignore them until high school. But if I become popular now, things will be easier when I get there."

I started to ask, "What happens to me if you become popular and I don't?" But I stopped myself. Because honestly? I was afraid of the answer.

CHAPTER NINE

Before the first bell on Monday, Tori and I stood at our locker, listening to the latest Taylor Swift song on her phone with the volume only about halfway up.

"Stop with that garbage," Preston Williams, an eighth grader, said as he walked past us. "It's making my ears bleed."

"Girls wouldn't know good music if it slapped them in the face," his friend Aaron added. "So stupid."

Preston's a big kid with thick, curly brown hair and the bushiest eyebrows I've ever seen on another person. I'm not saying that's good or bad; it's just a fact. Aaron is tall and skinny and always wears shorts and T-shirts, even if it's cold and raining outside.

"Did he just call us stupid?" Tori asked after they'd gone. "Aaron Adams, the guy who told Mr. McCarthy that the earth is actually flat and people have been lying to us for hundreds of years?"

I shut our locker door. "I think he really likes attention. Or something. All right, you ready?"

"Let's do it," she said.

We were going to try out a new plan to get past the boys

we'd nicknamed the tripping boys, otherwise known as Jerrod and Rusty. Our locker was at the end of A hall, near the door that leads out to the parking lot. The other two halls, B and C, were parallel to ours. We'd tried once to go outside and then back in one of the other doors leading to another hall to avoid passing by the tripping boys, but the doors were locked for security reasons. We had to knock on the window really hard to get someone to notice us and let us back in.

If you've never been to a middle school before, I don't know how to even describe how crowded the halls get during passing time. Sometimes I imagine my younger self yelling, "Too many onions!" as I ate my mom's homemade chicken noodle soup. I couldn't get a single bite without a bit of onion and I did not like that. At all. Middle school hallways are like that—can't take a single step without running into someone.

Today we were going to try walking along the opposite end of the hall, as far away as possible from Jerrod and Rusty. We'd tried dodging them before, but they'd managed to dart over in front of us and not let us pass without making it difficult. It was like a game to them. Well, Tori and I were ready for the game to be over.

"Excuse me," I said over and over as we weaved in and out of people standing at their lockers. The five-minute bell rang, and I watched Jerrod and Rusty as they peered down the hallway, trying to spot us.

"Hurry," Tori said, her hand tightly gripping my arm.

"Sorry," I said as I bumped into someone. "Excuse us."

I heard Jerrod yell, "There they are!"

I grabbed Tori's hand and rushed to the middle of the hallway where I started to run. Yes, there were lots of onions, but too bad; they could move or get run over.

"Hey, girls, hold on there," said a loud, deep voice. I stopped in my tracks and turned around to find the principal glaring at us. He was probably in search of girls to send home because of the new dress code. "No running in the halls. You know better than that."

"Sorry," we both said.

Tori started to explain. "It's just—"

But he didn't let her finish. "No excuses. Those are the rules. Now please *walk* to your class, understand?"

We both nodded and hung our heads as we continued on.

"At least we didn't get tripped today," Tori said.

I leaned into her as we walked. "Way to look at the bright spot, I guess."

Outside the door of homeroom, Preston and Aaron were talking. I didn't look their way because I really didn't want to hear more insults from them.

"You're such a wuss," I heard Preston tell Aaron. "Come on. Man up."

I couldn't help but wonder what they were talking about. Man up about what? I didn't like that phrase. What did it even mean, to man up? To act like a man? To be tough?

Why is being tough a thing to be admired, though? And why is that something boys should be, anyway?

When we got to our seats, Tori turned around and said, "I think this school has a problem."

"What kind of problem?" I asked.

"A jerk problem," she replied.

The bell rang so she turned back around. I thought about Ben's "Private Property." About boys thinking that what's most important about a girl is how she looks to others. Then I pulled out my spiral notebook and wrote a haiku.

> Stars in the darkness.
> Why do we admire them?
> Not because they're tough.

The vice principal, Ms. Carson, came over the loud speaker for morning announcements.

"Good morning, everyone, and happy October! I hope you had a good weekend. A student this morning asked about wearing costumes on Halloween, and our policy is that you may dress up but there are to be no masks. We must be able to see your face. Furthermore, you cannot carry a weapon of any kind. And yes, that includes lightsabers."

Some of the students in my class laughed.

"I also want to remind you that the talent show is scheduled for December 18. Ms. Holland, who is in charge of organizing it, has hung a sign-up sheet outside her classroom. If you want to participate, you can sign up this coming Friday. Each and every performance must be approved by Ms. Holland, so keep that in mind. All right, that's all for now. Have a wonderful day of learning, students."

Tori turned around, silently clapping her hands and mouthed, "Talent show!"

I gave her a thumbs-up even though there was no way I was going to get up on a stage in front of people at this school.

As our homeroom teacher, Ms. Beaty, began class, I flipped to the last page of my notebook. My doodle page. I'd drawn pictures of flowers, trees, a kitty cat. And positive little sayings to try and get me through the hard days.

> You got this
> Be happy
> Girls rule

But I'd written other things, too.

> Life is hard
> Growing up sucks

Today I wrote:

> I miss my old school. A LOT!

CHAPTER TEN

All day long, it felt like boys at school were watching me. Was I imagining it or was it real? What if they'd read things about me and were sizing me up to see if they were true? And was this how it was going to be from now on because I'd found that stupid notebook? So many questions, and I didn't have a single answer.

When I crossed paths with Ben between sixth and seventh period, I said hi like I normally do. And do you know what he said back?

"Hey, how's it going? You know, that shirt you're wearing, uh . . ."

I stopped walking and looked down, thinking I might have spilled something at lunch and not noticed. "What about it?"

"It's just . . . never mind. It's fine."

I tried to figure out what he was talking about. I was just wearing a plain, baby-blue T-shirt. Although when I'd put it on this morning, I had thought it felt a little tighter. That must be it. It was too tight.

"Gotta run," Ben said as I stood there, wishing I could

call my mom and ask her to bring a baggy sweatshirt for me to throw on.

I hated this. I hated that I had to think about all these things now. Why couldn't I wear what I wanted to wear without worrying about how it looked or what people would think or if it was something that would get me sent home? I missed the days when I never thought about any of that—when my body was just for running around, playing soccer, being a kid. How come it couldn't be that way forever?

With my mind going a mile a minute, all I could manage was "Yeah, okay."

Two more classes, I told myself. *You just have to make it through two more classes.*

I couldn't stop thinking about it. About any of it. Boys were going around looking at girls and writing things about them in a secret notebook. No matter how much I wanted to forget about it, I couldn't. I wanted to forget, believe me. Like, I really, *really* wanted to forget. Or to pretend I'd never seen it and simply wish away the awful stuff that was happening.

But I had seen it. I knew something probably no other girl in our school knew. Something bad. And the longer I carried the secret, the heavier it got. It was like carrying around a bag I couldn't put down while people kept adding rocks to it.

When I got home, I went straight to Pip's box and

picked him up. He raised his head just slightly, and I swear his eyes looked right into mine.

"Aw," I whispered. "I'm happy to see you, too."

I held him close to my chest for a minute and felt myself relax for the first time all day. And while it was nice, I couldn't take a tortoise to school to comfort me every time something upsetting happened. If only.

So how was I supposed to live like this for the next three years?

And that's when I knew: I had to get that notebook. If I knew it wasn't circulating anymore, at least I'd have one less thing to worry about.

The question was, how?

"Everything all right?"

I spun around to find Mom standing in the doorway to my room. "Just giving Pip a hug."

She sniffled a little, pretending to be sad. "When hugging a turtle is preferable to hugging your mother, I suppose that means you're growing up."

I put Pip back in his box and then went over to my mom and wrapped my arms around her. "See? I can hug both my mom *and* a turtle."

She gave me a tight squeeze. "Oh, good." After I pulled away, she asked, "How was school today?"

Like always, I replied, "Fine." And then I quickly changed the subject. "What did Mr. Buck say when you called him? Or did Dad call him?"

"Actually, we both tried," Mom said. "But the secretary wouldn't put us through. She said we could email her with our thoughts because she was gathering parents' comments and then she would forward them to Mr. Buck at the end of the week so he could read through everything all at once."

"Do you believe her?" I asked.

She paused before she said, "I believe she'll gather the comments and pass them on. I'm not so sure I believe that he'll read and consider them. That's why a phone conversation would have been so much better. I really wanted to make sure he heard what we have to say, you know?"

"So what now?"

She shook her head. "I'm not sure. Maybe I'll write out my thoughts and send them to both him and the school board members, since they're the ones who approved the policy. That's probably better, anyway."

"Good idea," I said. "I'm gonna change, and then can I put Pip on the floor for some exercise? I promise I'll watch him."

"Sure, but why are you changing?" she asked.

"I think this shirt is too small," I said. "I need to go through my closet and get rid of some stuff. Is that okay?"

She tilted her head and narrowed her eyes. "Hazel. Did something happen? Did someone say something about your shirt?"

I shook my head. "It just feels too tight, okay? And I

don't want to talk about it. You didn't answer my question. Can I let Pip out for a little while?"

She looked like she had more questions, but luckily she didn't ask. "Actually, we need to get ready to take him to the vet. Our appointment is in a half hour. We'll get him checked out, make sure he's healthy, and find out how old he is."

"Okay, are we leaving now?"

"In a few minutes. I suppose you can let him out while I get us both a snack. Let me go and do that."

"Sounds good. Oh, I forgot to tell you, Tori said she'd ask Jeanie if she could put up a sign at the vet's office about Pip. Maybe we'll find someone that way?"

"Wonderful," Mom said. "If you make me one, I can hang it in the coffee shop, too."

"Okay." I paused. "Mom, maybe I should keep him. I mean, would it be so terrible to have a nice turtle for the rest of my life?"

"Honey, there may be someone out there who has been dreaming of a pet tortoise forever. You could make that dream come true. And if it doesn't happen, if you can't find anyone, how about we revisit it then? Sound fair?"

I nodded. "Yeah. That's fair."

After Mom left, I put a towel from my hamper on the carpet and placed Pip on it. As I watched him slowly explore (*very* slowly, obviously), I could tell he was enjoying his freedom. The freedom to move around, to go wherever he wanted, and to not be confined to a box. The more I thought about it, the more I realized that's what I wanted. To move around freely at school and not worry that boys were secretly rating me in their heads. And I didn't want to be confined to a box, a box that said girls were good for one thing and one thing only: the way they looked.

I wasn't sure what to do about any of it. It seemed like such a big problem. An enormous problem, really. But there was one thing I could do that might help a little bit.

I needed to get that notebook from Ben and make sure no one ever saw it again. Somehow, some way, I had to do it.

It isn't easy
trying to do the right thing,
but no excuses.

At the exam, the vet told us Pip was four to five years old, so pretty young for a tortoise, and in very good health.

"Do you recall seeing him before?" my mom asked. "Since we found him in a parking lot, I was just wondering if someone around here left him there."

The vet shook his head. "Nope. Pretty sure this is his first time here. Maybe they were passing through town or something."

"Could be," my mom said. "Jeanie told us you agreed to let us hang a little sign about him out front. Thank you for that."

"Not a problem," he said. "We appreciate you taking care of him temporarily. It's a good thing you're doing."

I was glad to hear this. I'd been worried that the vet might think I was a terrible person for wanting to find a new home for Pip. It wasn't that I didn't want him. I did want him. Kind of.

Sometimes I think being twelve years old means being confused about everything all the time. That's how it feels to me, anyway.

CHAPTER ELEVEN

The next day, I told Tori I'd meet her at homeroom because I had something important I needed to do before school. Thankfully, she didn't ask for details. Ben's locker was in C hall, so I went there and waited for him to show up. I'd thought about what I'd say so I'd feel ready, but when he walked up, my mouth felt like I'd been eating dirt all morning. Not only that, but I was afraid my heart might explode from beating so hard.

"Hazel, you okay?" Ben asked as he dropped his backpack on the floor.

I swallowed hard. "Yeah, I was just wondering . . ."

I didn't finish. He stared at me. "Wondering what?"

Oh my gosh, why was this so difficult? "Um, yeah, I was wondering if I could, well, do you have a protractor I could borrow? I sort of . . . lost mine."

"Protractor?"

"Yeah. You know, for math class."

"You want to borrow my protractor."

I could feel sweat beading on the back of my neck. "Yes, please."

He shrugged. "Sure. I just have to find it. Haven't used it for a while."

My words came out fast. "That's why I figured you'd be a good person to ask, you know? Everyone in my class will be needing theirs, so they can't loan one to me."

He spun his lock around three times and jiggled his locker open. A lot of the girls have pictures and stickers on their locker doors, but Ben didn't have anything. What I noticed the most was the smell—like something rotten.

I plugged my nose. "Oh my gosh, Ben, has something died in there?"

He laughed. "Probably. I think there might be some cucumber slices that Mimi made me bring on the first day of school. It's like the start of every year is a new chance to start fresh and get it right, you know? Healthy snacks. Good homework habits. No more tardy slips. Then it all flies out the window after a couple of weeks." He rummaged around the messy pile of papers and books. I wasn't sure if he was looking for the cucumber or the protractor. "I should probably find it and throw it out, huh?"

"Ben, I'm not even joking when I say that you should do that before you do anything else."

He continued digging around while I searched for a glimpse of that notebook, but I didn't see it. Maybe it was in his backpack? And if so, was there a way I could get into it without him seeing me?

As he knelt down to look through the stack of stuff on

the bottom shelf, I started thumbing through books on the top shelf. I pulled a crumpled paper bag out and opened it. The smell about made me pass out.

"Found the cucumbers," I told him.

"Cool, thanks. Can you throw that away over there?" He waved toward a garbage can across the hall. As I made my way to it, the bell rang. Disappointment filled me. There'd be no notebook for me this morning, only a smelly cucumber. Just my luck.

"I gotta go," I told Ben.

"Here," he said as he jumped to his feet. "I found it!" He handed me the protractor and turned back to his locker. "Good luck with that."

"Thanks," I said, feeling totally defeated.

"And thank you," he said, turning back to me. "Hopefully my locker won't smell like death anymore."

It was like a bad joke or one of those T-shirts about your grandma going on a fabulous vacation and all you got was a T-shirt. CAME FOR THE NOTEBOOK WITH ALL THE GIRLS' NAMES AND ALL I GOT WAS A BAG OF SMELLY CUCUMBER SLICES.

Oh, joy.

At lunch, Tori and I went to the library, as usual. We're lucky that Mrs. Thompson lets a few of us eat lunch in there to escape the cafeteria. There's an elevated area with two comfy sofas and a large table with games and puzzles stacked in the middle. I'm just happy to eat in peace and maybe write a haiku or two to slip in a book.

After I checked out a couple of books about tortoises, we climbed the three stairs and took our usual seats at the big table. Two other girls sat on one of the sofas, reading and munching on their sandwiches. As I started to unpack my lunch, I heard sniffling.

I turned around and saw a boy curled up, arms hugging his knees, against the shelf of picture books that some of the Language Arts teachers like to use in their classes. His face was buried in his arms so all I could see was his curly black hair. I looked at Tori, hoping she'd run over to ask the boy what was wrong. I know I could have done it, but I'm not very good at that kind of thing. The last thing I wanted was to upset him even more. Still, when someone is crying, you should check on them. Shouldn't you?

Thankfully, Tori knows me. She gave me an understanding nod before she got up, went down the steps, and sat down next to him. I wanted to hear what was going on, so after a minute, I followed her and joined them on the floor.

"What's wrong?" Tori asked. "Do you need help with something?"

He wiped his face across the sleeve of his shirt, then shook his head before ducking back down into his arms.

"Come on," Tori said. "We want to help. Can you talk to us? Please? We're super nice, honest. Oh, and I'm Tori and this is Hazel. What's your name?"

He raised his head and sniffled. "Dion. And don't y'all go and tell people you saw me crying. It'll just make things worse."

"We won't," I said. "We'd never do that."

"My moms say boys should cry more often," Tori said matter-of-factly. "That the world needs more sensitive men. Or something like that."

Dion sniffled again. "Tell that to the bullies of the world."

"Is someone hurting you?" Tori asked softly, her voice filled with concern. "Because that is not okay. At all."

"I just . . ." He sighed. "I don't fit in anywhere. I miss my old school. I miss . . ." He looked around like he wanted to make sure no one could hear him before he whispered, "I miss recess."

I'd never felt so sure in such a short amount of time that I would soon have a new friend. Before I could say, "I feel the exact same way," Tori said, "I know it's hard at first, but it's going to be okay. We just have to figure out a way to get in with the right crowd."

I knew Tori was trying to be helpful, but I flinched. What if there never was the right crowd for people like Dion and me? What then?

"I'm sorry," I told him. "I know it's hard. I don't remember you from Hoover Elementary. Which school did you go to?"

"You wouldn't know it," he said. "We moved here over the summer. All the way from Alabama."

So he wasn't just new to middle school; he was new to our town—and our whole *state*.

"Why'd you move?" Tori asked.

"My grandpop died, and my grandma begged us to come and live with her. They've lived here in Willow a long time. Anyway, we're living in her big, old house with her now and she's really glad to have us. My pop found a job at the hardware store, but my mama's a teacher and she hasn't found anything permanent yet, so she's subbing."

"Hey, someday you could have her as a teacher, then!" I said. "That could be . . . interesting."

"I hope I don't," he said. "I don't want to call my mama Mrs. Wise!"

My stomach growled. "Did you bring your lunch? Want to come up to the table and eat with us?"

"You guys eat in here?" he asked.

"For now," Tori said. "Hazel really likes it in here. Hopefully we'll give the cafeteria another try one of these days."

I knew Tori was getting kind of tired of eating in the library. She wanted to be in the cafeteria where she could be seen. Where she could try to sit with the popular kids. It gave me a stomachache just thinking about trying the cafeteria again.

"I already ate my sandwich," Dion said. "Still hungry, though. And I have soccer practice after school."

I smiled. "Hey, we play soccer, too! We practice Wednesdays and Thursdays, though."

Dion looked around again. He seemed so frightened that someone would see him. Probably because it wasn't cool to hang out with girls or something. Who made all these stupid rules, anyway? People are always so happy to judge other people about what they're doing without thinking about why. I don't get it.

Dion got to his feet, so Tori and I did the same. Once we were sitting at the table, Tori didn't hesitate, just handed him half her sandwich. I opened my bag of grapes and set them between us so we could share.

"Thanks," Dion said as he took a grape. "I really mean it. Thanks a lot."

"No problem," Tori said. "Hazel and I were saying earlier that this school has a jerk problem."

That made Dion smile and boy, did he have a nice smile. "A jerk problem. I guess that's one way to put it."

"What would you call it?" I asked.

"I dunno. There's definitely . . . something. Seems like maybe people are afraid to be real? I mean, just to be themselves, you know? Like, it's all about looking good for everyone else. Gotta be this way or that way, or else."

I opened my notebook and started writing.

Dion raised his eyebrows. "You taking down my brilliance?"

"She writes little poems," Tori said.

"Haiku," I explained.

"That's cool," he said. "I like poetry. My pop used to read that book *Where the Sidewalk Ends* to me when I was a little kid. He used to say, 'There's a poet inside all of us, Dion. I want you to remember that.' What do you think he meant, exactly?"

I wrote while Tori talked. "I think poets are good at seeing the world in an interesting way. Maybe he meant we can all be like that if we try?"

Dion nodded. "Yeah. Maybe so." He looked at me. "Can we hear your haiku?"

> Roses bloom in lots
> of colors, never worried
> about fitting in.

"Haiku are usually about nature," I explained after I read it. "I do them about lots of things, though."

"I like it," Dion said as he took more grapes. "It's so true, too. Roses just gonna do what they're meant to do. They don't care a bit about what people think. And no one gets mad at a yellow rose because it's not red. They just let it be and move on. How come people can't be that way all the time?"

Tori and I didn't say anything. We didn't have an answer for him.

"Dion?" I said.

"Yeah?"

"You can eat lunch with us here tomorrow if you want," I told him.

"Yeah," Tori said. "Any time, actually."

"Thanks," he said. "I really mean it. Again."

I wanted to ask him if he'd written in a secret notebook being passed around by boys at school. But part of me didn't want to know the answer, in case it was yes. I wanted to hold on to the Dion I knew right now—the boy who liked poetry and cried because his feelings were hurt.

"You're very polite," Tori told him.

"My mama taught me well, I guess," he said. "She's always saying, 'The world has enough turkeys, so don't be a turkey. Be a chickadee instead. Sweet and harmless. That's what the world needs.'"

"I think I like your parents," I told him as I tossed my trash into my lunch bag. And that's when the greatest idea ever popped into my head.

"Hey, do you like tortoises?" I asked.

CHAPTER TWELVE

Dion's grandma had an old dog at their house, so the tortoise wouldn't work for him. I was so disappointed. It would have been the perfect solution. He was really nice about it, but it made me feel like I had no idea what I was doing and if I'd ever be able to find Pip a good home. But maybe that wouldn't be so bad.

The thing was, all day long I found myself looking forward to going home and seeing Pip. He gave me something new to think about. Something good. I liked having to care for him. He needed me in a way that no one else did and it felt nice. Plus, he didn't care about being popular or not, didn't care what I wore or what I looked like, and he really didn't care if my shirt was a little too small. He was the most nonjudgmental turtle I'd ever met.

Mom had specifically told me not to get too attached, but that was exactly what was happening, and I didn't know how to stop it. Or even if I wanted to. Maybe he was better off staying with me. Maybe it wouldn't be so bad to have just one pet the rest of my life. Millions of people have just one spouse their entire life and that seems to work out pretty well.

I'd never really understood what "I feel so torn" meant until now, but it was pretty much how I felt. Torn. Torn between wanting to keep him and finding him the perfect home where he would be happy and loved forever.

As I headed toward my bike after school, I saw Ben coming right for me in the main hallway.

He smiled as he said, "Hazel, that protractor work okay for you?"

"Oh, yeah, thanks so much," I said, watching as he tried to put a stack of books into his backpack. He stopped walking and pulled something out in order to get the others in. And that something was the notebook!

Think fast, I told myself. *This is your chance.*

I remembered a spy movie I watched with my dad awhile back. The spy wanted some important papers, so he ran right into the guy carrying them, forcing him to drop his briefcase. Then, in a split second, the spy switched briefcases. He did it so fast and so sneakily, the other guy didn't even realize what had happened.

With no other ideas, I pretended to jump out of the way as a group of kids walked by, which basically resulted in me throwing myself at Ben, knocking him over and me tumbling after him.

He looked around, stunned, trying to figure out what had just happened. I reached for the notebook, but I wasn't quick enough. Ben grabbed it along with the other books and jumped to his feet.

"What was that?" he asked. I waited for him to offer to help me up, but he just stood there, his face getting angrier by the second.

"You like the young ones now, Robinson?" someone called out.

"Get a room!" someone else said.

Ben muttered a cuss word under his breath as I helped myself up.

"Sorry," I said. "I was trying to get out of the way and I, uh, lost my balance or something."

He glared at me. "That was more than losing your balance, Hazel."

I shook my head hard. "I'm so sorry. I don't really know what happened."

It was a lie, and I felt horrible about it. But I felt even more horrible about that notebook. The thing was, if I didn't hurry up and get it from him, he'd eventually pass it on to someone else again. I had to get it from him. I just had to.

I almost asked him about it. Like, I could have told him I'd peeked inside the notebook when I was at his house and had been disgusted by what I'd seen.

"Why?" I wanted to ask him. "Why are you passing that thing around?"

But I couldn't do it. I wanted to, except just thinking about confronting him made me feel like I might lose my lunch right there in the middle of the hallway. Because in my imagination, he'd yell at me and tell me it was none of my business. He'd tell me I was a silly sixth grader who didn't know anything and I was probably just jealous of the gorgeous girls who got good ratings.

I felt so mad. Mad at myself that I didn't have it in me and mad at Ben for starting the whole thing.

He zipped up his backpack. "I don't know what's going on, Hazel, but you better watch it. Okay?"

Great. Now it seemed like he was suspicious of me. Getting the notebook away from him suddenly seemed a hundred times harder. "Yeah. Sure. Okay." I smiled. "Again, I'm really sorry. See you later."

He seemed to relax a little. "Yeah. See ya."

When I got home, I lay on my bed with Pip on my chest.

I gently petted his shell as I thought about what to do next. It seemed like I had four choices:

1. Give up and let the notebook continue to be a thing.
2. Tell Ben I knew about it and ask him to give it to me so I could throw it in the trash.
3. Tell someone else about it so I could maybe have some help.
4. Figure out a way to get it from him at his house.

Giving up would have been the easiest thing to do. It was the choice my brain was arguing for. *It's too big of a problem*, it whispered to me. *You can't do this alone.*

If I decided to tell someone, hoping they'd help me, who would that be? There was no way it could be Tori. We had a few other friends we hung out with sometimes, but they were friends to both of us. What if someone decided to tell her what we were doing? She could get really upset with me, for a bunch of different reasons, and that was the last thing I wanted.

The two best choices seemed to be to either find a big tub of courage and slather myself with it so I could talk to Ben, or sneak into his room at home and steal it.

I'd already had the perfect opportunity to talk to Ben, though, and I'd blown my chance. If I hadn't managed to do it then, I was pretty sure I never would. That meant there was only one choice left. I was going to have to get into his room somehow, find the notebook, and take it.

I put Pip back in his box and texted Tori.

What are you having for dinner? We're having tuna casserole. So gross!

She texted back right away: **Mimi is making home-made pizza with spinach and stuff on it. It's good! You can come over and eat with us if you want.**

I responded: **Okay, I'll be there by 5:00.**

The way my stomach felt, I knew I wouldn't be able to eat much of anything. But it didn't matter. That's not why I was really going over there. While Ben ate his pizza, I'd excuse myself to the bathroom and that's when I'd grab the notebook from his room.

I rolled over and put Pip back in his box. I watched Pip as he nibbled on some green beans and carrots I'd put in there earlier. "Wish me luck," I whispered to him.

I guess tortoises are the strong but silent type.

CHAPTER THIRTEEN

"Come to my room," Tori said, taking my hand as soon as she opened the front door. "I have to show you something."

Her house smelled like popcorn. Must have been her afternoon snack. I think freshly popped popcorn must be one of the world's most wonderful scents. How do kids who work at movie theaters not just stand there and eat it all day long?

"Is everything okay?" I asked as I followed her into her room.

She grinned. "Oh my gosh, better than okay. I'm *so* excited right now, you have no idea."

I took a seat on her bed. "Okay, you gonna tell me or do I have to guess a hundred times and never get it right?"

"Remember how my karaoke machine broke and I was super upset because I didn't want to wait for Christmas to get another one?"

"Yeah?"

"Mimi found one at the thrift store for five bucks!" She pulled the machine out from her closet. "It's a little beat up, but it still works."

I pointed to the dome on top. "What's that?"

She held her finger up, like she was telling me to wait, while she plugged it in. Green lights twinkled on the wall. "Disco lights!" she squealed.

Tori's dream is to be like her idol P!nk someday. And it may happen because she has *such* a good voice.

She plopped down next to me. "I'm so happy! Now I can start practicing for the talent show. If I can just decide on a song. Will you help me figure out what to sing?"

I looked at her. "You really want to do that?"

"Do what?"

"The talent show?"

"Why wouldn't I?"

"Maybe because our school has a jerk problem, and they might be jerks about your singing?"

"Hazel, are you saying my singing is bad?"

I laughed nervously. "No! That's not what I meant. I love your singing, you know that. It's just . . ."

She didn't let me finish. "Ben's done it the last two years, and he's never had any troubles."

"Yeah, but he's a boy."

"So?"

Right then, I wished it was anyone else but her brother who had the notebook. I wanted to tell her *so* badly. She was my best friend. I should have been able to tell her anything and everything.

"So, boys have an easier time, usually. Don't they?"

"Dion was crying in the library," she pointed out. "Pretty sure he wasn't having an easy time."

I didn't know what to say to that. Was I wrong to be worried about her? To want to protect her from people saying mean things?

"I'll work hard," she said. "It'll be good. No, wait. Better than good. I know you don't see it the same way, but I think if I work hard and prove myself, this could give me a lot of points."

"Points?"

"Yeah. Points with girls like Maddie Gray and Dawn Jones, that cute and funny seventh grader I have in study hall. Everyone loves Dawn. I want to be like her. I just have to prove myself, you know?"

I'm not sure I'd ever felt as small as I felt in that moment. It seemed like she was telling me I wasn't enough. That no matter how good of a friend I was to her, I'd never be enough. She wanted more. Not just more, *a lot* more.

"Hey," she said, wiggling her eyebrows. "You want to be my backup dancer?"

"Tori, do you remember who you're talking to, exactly?"

She gave me a funny look. "What do you mean?"

"Have you seen me dance?" I hopped up, determined to be just as cute and funny as Dawn Jones, and started doing the sprinkler in the middle of her room, one arm folded behind my head and my other arm straight out in front of me as I hopped around.

Laughing, she said, "Wait, you need some music!"

She turned on her karaoke machine and a Katy Perry song started playing.

I danced even harder.

Tori laughed and laughed while I kept making a fool of myself. Why couldn't this be enough? Tori and me, just like it'd always been.

She got up to dance too and even though part of me wanted to cry, there was also a part of me that knew she loved me a whole lot, that I was a part of her family and she was a part of mine, and we had something special. I had to believe that nothing could ever change that.

She held my hands as she continued to laugh hysterically and spun me around and around.

"You'd be the best backup dancer ever," she told me.

Before I could answer, her brother burst through the door. "What's going on in here?"

Tori ran over and shoved him. "Hey, haven't you heard of knocking, Benjamin Buttercup?"

I sort of loved it when she called her brother *Benjamin Buttercup*. It almost made me wish I had a brother or a sister so I could come up with a funny name to call them.

"Okay, okay, sorry," Ben said. "Just wanted to see why you two were laughing so hard."

"I was showing Tori my awesome dance moves," I told him.

"Cool," he said. "Can I see?"

"No!" we both yelled at the same time.

"You're no fun," he said. "Fine. See ya later."

"Where are you going?" I asked, hoping this might be my chance to get that stupid notebook away from him.

He gave me a funny look. "To my room?"

"So, you'll be here for the spinach pizza?" I asked.

"Yes. Where else would I be? I live here, don't I?"

"Yeah, I just thought . . . Never mind."

"Bye!" Tori pushed him out and shut the door. "Come on," she said. "I'll sing with the karaoke machine and you dance."

"In your room, fine," I said. "But not at school in front of a million people."

She rolled her eyes. "A million people? I wish."

How could my best friend and I be so different? She loved attention, while I did everything possible to avoid it.

"Dinner's ready!" Alice called.

"Too bad," I teased. "No more sprinkler dancing."

"After dinner!" Tori said. "You can stay, can't you?"

I couldn't tell her it all depended on whether or not I could steal her brother's personal property.

CHAPTER FOURTEEN

The spinach pizza was delicious. I couldn't believe it. Alice had made it on a pizza crust flavored with herbs, put three different cheeses on it, and then topped it with spinach leaves that got crunchy in the oven.

I took a couple of bites and then I knew I had to make my move. Ben was a fast eater; if I didn't hurry, he'd be finished with his meal before I had a chance to get into his room.

"Sorry, I have to use the restroom," I said as I took my napkin off my lap and set it on the table.

"That's fine, sweetie," Jeanie said with a smile.

I hurried to the hallway and carefully opened Ben's door and ducked inside.

My eyes scanned the room, past the shelf with baseball trophies, his unmade bed, and the floor littered with dirty clothes. I stepped over a pair of boxer shorts (ew!) and walked over to his desk. There were papers and books covering the top, but the notebook was nowhere in sight. Where could it be?

I turned and looked around the room again. I had about one more minute before they'd start to get suspicious. It had to be here somewhere, it just had to be.

And then I saw his backpack. He probably hadn't emptied it. I rushed over, unzipped it, and looked inside. My heart was beating so loudly, I almost shushed it, worried everyone could hear it from the other room. I quickly pulled the notebook out and read the words that had caught my attention the first time: PRIVATE PROPERTY OF BEN R.

Was I really doing this? Was I *stealing* something? I almost dropped it and ran out of there, ready to pretend none of this had ever happened. But this was my chance. My one chance to stop the notebook from getting around at our school some more.

I walked toward the door and then I realized I still had a problem. A big one. How would I get it out of the house? Should I slide it up my shirt and leave now, making up an excuse? Or should I hide it somewhere and make sure to get it before I left later on?

I decided it was too risky to leave right then. They'd look me over hard if I told them I was sick, maybe even make me lie down. If I had a notebook hidden in my shirt, they'd notice for sure. No, I had to hide it in the house somewhere and then grab it right before I rushed out the door for home.

Was there some place safe in Tori's room? Or was the bathroom the best bet? By now, everyone had to be wondering what was taking me so long. I had to hurry.

The bathroom made the most sense because it was the

only way I could get into a room by myself with no one watching me. I hurried in and placed the notebook in the bathtub behind the shower curtain. It felt wrong to have it so visible, though, so I grabbed a clean towel from underneath the sink and threw it on top of the notebook.

There. Done. And now I just had to cross my fingers that no one had a sudden urge to bathe in the next thirty minutes.

I went back to the table and took my seat, trying hard not to look like the guilty thief I'd become.

"A thousand pieces is too hard," Tori was saying. "The last one we did was five hundred pieces and it still took us, like, two weeks." She turned to me. "Mimi got a puzzle at the thrift store along with my karaoke machine."

"What's the picture on it?" I asked.

"It's a Paris balcony," Alice explained. "A gorgeous Paris balcony. Wait, maybe all Paris balconies are gorgeous. Anyway, it's on the coffee table. You can take a look after you finish your dinner."

"Yeah, I love how it looks," Tori said. "I just wish it wasn't a thousand pieces."

"It's a puzzle," Ben said. "It's not supposed to be easy."

"No, but it shouldn't be too hard, either," Tori argued. "Otherwise it'll sit there and no one will work on it and instead of something fun it turns into something that just makes people miserable."

"Okay, little Miss Sunshine," Ben said as he stood up with his empty plate. "Whatever you say."

Ben was already finished. That meant he might go in his room, look in his backpack, and notice that the notebook was gone. I had to get out of there before that happened.

After he stepped into the kitchen, I said, "Um, I'm really sorry, but I don't feel well. I think I need to go home."

Both of Tori's moms looked at me with worried faces. "Oh dear," Alice said. "My cooking isn't that bad, is it?"

"No, it's really good," I said. "I'm not sure what's wrong. Just think I need to go home and lie down."

"Of course," Jeanie said. "Do you want one of us to drive you?"

"No, that's okay."

"We can put your bike in the back of the truck; it's not a problem," Alice said.

I shook my head. "No, I'm just gonna, um, use the bathroom one more time and then I'll head home. I'll be okay, honest. I think the fresh air will feel good."

Jeanie and Alice looked at each other, and I knew they were trying to decide if they should stop me. If one of them insisted on taking me home, I'd have to leave the notebook here. There's no way I could sneak it out. By now I was kicking myself that I hadn't brought along a backpack or bag or something to help me get the thing out of there.

I held my breath waiting to see what they were going to say.

"Do you have your phone with you?" Jeanie asked.

I patted my pocket. "Yes."

"All right. Sure hope you feel better."

"Thanks," I said. I turned to Tori. "Sorry. We'll have to try out that new karaoke machine another time."

"No problem," Tori said.

I took my plate to the kitchen and then headed for the bathroom. When I found the door locked, panic rushed through me. What if Ben found the notebook in the bathroom? What would he say to me? What would he *do* to me?

I didn't know what to do. Where to go. I could feel sweat dripping down my back. Well, at least now I probably looked truly sick.

Just as I was about to run out of the house and never show my face again, Ben opened the door. When he saw me standing there, he smiled. "You need it again?" he asked.

I could barely speak. "Not feeling too good," I managed.

"Oh. Sorry," he said.

As soon as he'd gone into his room and shut the door, I rushed in, grabbed the notebook, shoved it under my shirt, and raced toward the front door.

"See you later," I called out. "Thanks for having me."

"Bye!" Tori called out.

"Feel better!" Alice said.

I got on my bike and flew. Like, I'm pretty sure if a peregrine falcon had shown up and decided to fly beside me, I would have beaten it home.

I couldn't believe it. I'd done it. The notebook was mine now.

CHAPTER FIFTEEN

"Hi, Hazel!" Mom called out when she heard the front door open. They may have had tuna casserole, but the house smelled like warm bread and cheese. My stomach rumbled. "Did you have a nice time?"

"Yes!" I called out. "I want to check on Pip. I'll be there in a minute."

When I got to my room, I shut the door and pulled out the notebook. My hands shook as I held it, thinking about all the girls' names written on the pages.

I shoved it under my pillow to deal with later and then went and said hello to Pip. "I did it," I whispered. "Aren't you proud of me?"

I'm pretty sure he gave me the tiniest of nods to tell me he was *very* proud of me. I picked him up and carried him out to the family room where Mom and Dad were watching a show together.

"I thought you'd be a little later," Mom said.

I just shrugged and hoped that would be enough. I didn't want to lie to them about what happened. "I'm going to put Pip down and let him roam while I practice my flute. Okay?"

"Sure," Mom said.

"Any luck finding him a home?" Dad asked as he paused whatever show they'd been watching.

"Not yet," I said as I grabbed some newspaper from the pile on the counter. Luckily, I had a dad who liked to read the actual paper every morning instead of just his phone. "I thought this one kid at school would be good for Pip, but they have a dog. I was really bummed because he would have been perfect. But I don't want Pip to be a midnight snack or something."

"You know, here's another idea," Dad said. "Turtle soup is supposed to be really delicious."

I set Pip down, stood up, and crossed my arms. "Dad! Stop it. That's not nice."

He smiled. "You know I'm teasing."

"A couple more weeks and then we may need to change strategies," Mom said.

I didn't like the sound of that. I went and took a seat beside her. "What do you mean?"

"I mean," she said, "the longer you keep him, the more attached you're going to get. I don't want it to be too hard to say goodbye. So if a viable option doesn't come up soon, it may be time to contact the Reptile Man or other people like him."

"But, Mom—"

She didn't let me finish. "I know it's not what you want, honey. But he'd take good care of him. It's his job, after all."

"That doesn't mean it's what's best, though," I said. "You know I'd rather keep Pip forever than do that."

Why did this have to be so difficult? Why couldn't I find the perfect solution? Next to getting that awful notebook from Ben, it was all I wanted in life.

As I sat there pouting, I noticed a pad of paper on Mom's lap filled with her messy handwriting. I could make out only a few things—*EEOC*, *discrimination*, and *promotion*.

"Mom?" I asked as I tapped her notes with my finger. "Is everything all right?"

She quickly flipped the cover over. "Everything's fine." She turned to me with a smile as she tucked a strand of hair behind my ear. "Just boring grown-up stuff."

"I think it's okay to tell her, Kate," Dad said.

"But I don't want her to worry," Mom replied.

I really didn't like it when they talked about me like I wasn't there. "Hello? I'm sitting right here. And I can take it. I'm in the sixth grade. Maybe you should walk the halls of a middle school and hear all the things kids talk about. Wait. Don't do that. I don't want you to die from shock."

Both of them laughed. "You want to give us an example?" Dad asked.

"Absolutely not," I said.

"Okay, then," he said. "Does that make you feel better, Kate? I think she can handle it."

Before I could say anything, Mom spoke quickly. "Hazel, I'm going to tell you, but you can't tell anyone else, okay? It needs to stay between us. I was, um, passed over for a promotion at work even though I have a lot more experience. So, I've filed a claim with the Equal Employment Opportunity Commission. That's all. It's nothing for you to worry about, okay?"

"Who got the job instead of you?" I asked.

"Oh, um," she paused. "Geoffrey got it. He's now the day supervisor."

Mom had worked at the Beanery for as long as I could remember, and it seemed like I knew just about everyone who worked there. I think Geoffrey was the last name I'd expected to hear.

"What?" I gasped. "How long has he been there? Like, six months or something?"

"Seven, actually, but yes. Now that you're older, I felt like I could take on more responsibility. And then, they just passed right over me."

"Why?" I asked. "Why would they do that?"

"Well," Mom said, "have you ever noticed I've only had male supervisors?"

I thought about it for a second and realized she was right. "You think you didn't get it because you're a woman?"

"That's exactly what she thinks," Dad said. "And why she's filed a complaint. Looks a lot like discrimination to me. You know what that is, right, Hazel?"

"Kind of? I think? I mean, if you're looking for a definition, I'm not a walking dictionary," I said. "I wish I was, though. Push a button and out comes the perfect definition. That'd be so cool."

Mom grabbed her phone and asked Siri, "What's *discrimination* mean?"

Oops. Forgot about Siri. Sorry, Siri.

She gave us this definition: "The unjust or prejudicial treatment of different categories of people or things, especially on the grounds of race, age, or sex."

"So, unfair treatment based on a certain category," I said. "Like, being treated unfairly because you're a woman."

"Yes," Mom said matter-of-factly.

And just like that, I had a lot more in common with my mother than I'd thought.

CHAPTER SIXTEEN

When it was bedtime, I took Pip back to my room. Before I went to the bathroom to wash my face and brush my teeth, I sat on my bed as I held him.

"I don't know what to do," I said. "Mom obviously doesn't want to keep you. Do I try to talk her into it? And if so, how? Or do I just need to work harder to find the perfect place for you?"

I told myself I was tired and that was probably making everything feel extra horrible. So I put him in his box and went to the bathroom to get ready for bed.

When I finally crawled under the covers, I grabbed the book I'd been reading since I'd finished my last read through of *Pippi Longstocking*. The book was *Front Desk* by Kelly Yang, and I was excited to get back to it. One thing about books? They give you someone else's problems to think about instead of your own, and that's strangely comforting.

Except as I read, I couldn't stop thinking about the notebook under my pillow.

Specifically, what did it say about me?

You don't want to know, I told myself.

But part of me did want to know. I wished it didn't. I wished I wasn't dying of curiosity. I also wished I knew what to do with the thing. I didn't really want to keep it. But I didn't want to get rid of it, either. Not yet, anyway. Because maybe one day I'd wake up brave enough to march into the principal's office and tell him about the jerk problem we had at our school. It might not happen until the very last day of eighth grade, but it could happen. Maybe.

I tried to read my novel. I really did. But every third or fourth sentence it was like someone had a large, sharp stick and was poking my brain.

You're probably in there.

What does it say?

You can't avoid it forever.

Get it over with. Right now.

Do it!

Just as I started to pull it out from underneath my pillow, there was a knock on my door.

"Come in," I said.

Mom stepped in and said, "Can I talk to you for a minute?"

"Yeah."

I moved over and she sat down on the edge of the bed. "I just want to make sure you don't have any more questions about . . . what we were talking about earlier."

"The only thing I'm wondering is whether you could lose your job over it."

"I suppose I could, but that would be illegal."

"Were you scared to file the claim?"

"Of course I was. But I knew it was the right thing to do. They need to know it's wrong. It may not help me, but maybe it will help someone else down the road."

Wow. Another superpower. I was beginning to think my mom was actually a superhero disguised as a wife and mother.

"I want to be that brave," I told her. "I could never do something like that."

She reached out and took my hand. "Sweetheart, this is how I think of it when it comes to things like this. White women couldn't vote until 1920. And black women couldn't vote until very recently, 1965. My grandmother couldn't even apply for a credit card in her own name. Banks wouldn't even lend them money on their own. Do you know why those things changed?"

I shook my head.

"Because women fought for those rights. They fought really hard. And I'm pretty certain that the best way to show our appreciation to those women is to continue fighting today when we see something that's unfair. Do you think those women weren't scared?"

I dropped my mom's hand and hugged my knees to my chest. "How am I supposed to know?"

"Well, yes, it's hard to know exactly how they felt, but my guess is that they were probably very frightened. I imagine they found strength in each other and knew that ultimately, it would change the lives of millions of women forever. And so they did what they believed was right, despite the fear." She leaned in. "Hazel, I know you are young and a bit shy and sensitive, but please, always remember you have a voice. And you have just as much of a right to use it as anyone else. Okay?"

I knew my mother well enough to know that the only answer she would accept was the one I gave her. "Okay."

"I found a quote I really love the other day," she said. "I think you'll like it. Ready?"

"Ready."

"It goes, 'Watch the turtle. He only moves forward by sticking his neck out.' Louis Gerstner Jr. said that. And women have to keep sticking their necks out if they want change."

"Should I stop calling you Mom and start calling you Turtle instead?"

She laughed. "No, thank you." She leaned in and kissed my cheek. "I love you. Sleep tight. See you in the morning."

"Good night."

She made it sound so easy. *Use your voice, that's what it's there for. You have as much right as anyone else.* Well, yeah, of course she's gonna say that, *because she's my mom*!

It was already nine-thirty and that meant time for me to go to sleep. But it seemed like I'd never be able to do that until I just opened the notebook and looked for my name.

So that's what I did. I got it out and flipped the pages.

Name after name after name. I didn't let myself stop to read what they'd written. I didn't want to see the words. I didn't want to look at a girl at school and let those comments be the first thing that popped into my brain. Girls have enough trouble being judged for things they have no control over; they didn't need one more thing shaping how someone saw them.

I was just about to the end and I felt myself relax because maybe I wasn't in there, after all. Maybe I'd been worried for nothing.

But on the second to last page, there it was:

HAZEL WALLACE
T.E. 3 there's a reason people call her camel lips
J.J. not even worth a rating
V.R. 1 uuuuuugly
P.W. 4 eh, she'd be all right if she lost a little weight
A.A. 2 LITERALLY THE WORST
B.R. NO COMMENT

I slammed the book shut as tears welled up in my eyes. There were more, but I couldn't read them. I started to throw it across the room but stopped myself. The last thing I needed was Mom coming in, seeing me upset, and asking me to explain what was going on.

How could people be so mean? How?

I put the notebook under my pillow and picked up *Front*

Desk. I should have turned out the light and tried to sleep, but I knew I'd just toss and turn. So I'd have to read until I couldn't keep my eyes open any longer.

The main character of the story, Mia, was also dealing with mean people. It probably wouldn't make me feel better, because I wasn't sure anything would make me feel better in that moment.

But at least I wouldn't feel so alone.

CHAPTER SEVENTEEN

The next day, Tori could see I wasn't my normal self.

"I'm tired," I told her. "I didn't sleep well."

"Are you sick?" she asked.

I'd almost forgotten about last night. "Maybe. My stomach still hurts."

Which was the truth. How could anyone read such hurtful things and *not* have a stomachache?

She smiled. "Well, I have just the thing to cheer you up. I figured out how you can be in the talent show with me."

"Tori, Taylor Swift coming to our school to perform would cheer me up. But *me* getting onstage and performing? You know I could never do that."

She smiled. "Sure you can! Wait until you hear my idea. I was thinking—"

"Tori!"

"Please, just listen, okay? I was thinking while I sang, you could do the lyrics to the song in sign language. Wouldn't that be awesome? And beautiful. Plus, if any hearing-impaired people are in the audience, they wouldn't feel left out."

"Sign language? Me?"

She shrugged. "Yeah. You could learn. I'd learn, too. We could do it together! Please, Hazel? You don't have to give me an answer right now. I'm going to sign up Friday, once I figure out the song I'm doing, and it's probably fine if we add you later."

It felt like my best friend and I were living on different planets. All she could think about was the talent show, something fun and happy-making. Meanwhile, all I could think about were the horrible words I'd read in a notebook that I now had in my bedroom. A notebook that many boys knew about but only one girl—me—knew about.

If I'd had a magic lamp with a genie inside, I would have wished to switch problems with Tori. Because trying to decide on a song seemed a whole lot more fun than trying to decide what to do about a disgusting notebook.

As for Tori's request, the best option seemed to be to go along with it and make her think I was considering it. For now, anyway.

"Fine. I'll think about it."

She squealed and threw her arms around me. "Thank you, my dear, sweet BFF, thank you!"

As we hugged, I heard sniffles nearby. I let go and turned around. It was our friend Sasha, from soccer, getting into her locker.

"Hey, what's wrong?" I asked. "You okay?"

"Mr. Buck is sending me home," she said as she wiped

her face with the back of her hand. "Said my shirt isn't appropriate for school."

Her T-shirt read: INSTEAD OF BEING RACIST OR SEXIST, JUST BE QUIET.

"No way," Tori said. "For that? Seriously?"

"Right?" Sasha said. "My mom is so angry. She's on her way to pick me up. I think she's gonna try to talk to him, but I doubt it'll do any good. She said we might have to move if this is how it's going to be."

"I'm so sorry, Sasha," I said. "It's not right."

"No, it's not," Tori said.

The warning bell rang, which meant we needed to get to class. "Do you want us to stay with you until she gets here?" I asked.

Sasha shook her head. "No, it's okay. I'll be fine. I was just embarrassed, you know? He did it in front of a bunch of people and it just . . . I don't know. It shocked me."

I understood. Sometimes tears come not because you're sad but because you're so full of all kinds of feelings that *something* has to come out.

Tori and I headed to class, and we didn't even try to avoid the tripping boys this time. It just seemed easier today to take it. They came up behind us and kept kicking our feet, trying to make us lose our balance, but we held on to each other and managed to make it to the end of the hallway.

"Good job," Tori said as she gave me a high five.

"Do you think they'll ever get tired of it?" I asked. "They have to, right? Like, at some point there'll be something else they want to do."

"Something more obnoxious, you mean?"

That was a depressing thought. "Yeah. Probably. I wish someone would say something. Every day people see them doing it, and no one says a word. It's so frustrating."

"I know," Tori said.

"Maybe we should do something nice for them. Show them we're trying hard to get along with everyone. Bake them cupcakes or something."

It stopped Tori in her tracks. "What did you just say? I think I didn't hear right, because it sounded like you said we should bake those horrible boys some *cupcakes*."

"That's what I said."

We were almost to our class. The halls were still pretty crowded, so I figured we had a couple of minutes left.

"But why?" she asked, her face all scrunched up like I'd just shoved a dirty diaper at her. "Why would you want to do that?"

"I don't know. Nothing else has worked. Maybe being super nice would make them feel bad? Or something?"

"Good morning, girls," Ms. Beaty said. "Are you going to join us or are you hoping we'll have class in the hallway this morning?"

Tori walked through the doorway and I started to follow her when I felt a hand around my upper arm.

"Hazel," a stern voice said. A voice I recognized. A voice that did not sound happy. At all.

I turned around and smiled at Ben. "Oh, hey. How's it going?"

He kept his voice low, but he was obviously mad. "Where is it?"

I tried to act like he was speaking Russian and I had no idea what any of his words meant. "What? What do you mean?"

"Don't do that," he snarled. "Don't pretend. I know you took it. It's the only thing that makes any sense. You looked at it in the bathroom last weekend, didn't you? And then you decided you didn't want it circulating at school anymore, so you stole it."

"Stole what?"

As the bell rang, Ms. Beaty came over to the door and looked back and forth between Ben and me. "Hazel, is everything all right?"

Ben quickly let go of my arm. "Yes," I said. "Sorry. I'm coming."

I glanced back at Ben and gave him a little shrug, trying to look as innocent as possible. He had to believe me, or he'd keep bugging me about it.

As I took a seat, I noticed Tori talking to the girl who sat across the aisle from her. It seemed like maybe she hadn't even noticed her brother in the hallway with me.

But I had noticed. I'd noticed how mad Ben was and

how determined he'd been to get me to admit I'd taken the notebook. If he came around again, whatever he said, I couldn't get flustered. I had to stay calm and just keep saying it: "Ben, what are you talking about?"

You can do it, I told myself. *Actually, you have to do it.*

CHAPTER EIGHTEEN

I was happy to see Dion when he came to the library with his hot lunch. It was pizza day. I patted the chair next to me and he took a seat.

"Hi," I said. "You're here!"

"I'm here." He picked up his slice and took a bite. Then he nodded toward the piece of paper and pen in front of me. "More haiku?"

"Maybe," I said. "We'll see. So far everything I want to say would be way more than seventeen syllables. Like, girls should be allowed to wear whatever they want, it's a free country, why are you doing this to us, Mr. Buck?"

Tori chuckled. "I like it. Now just shrink it down into something poetic and . . ."

"Meaningful?" Dion said, finishing the sentence.

"Yes!" Tori said. "Exactly."

"You make it sound so easy," I said.

I reached into my lunch bag and took out the bag of grapes and set them in the middle of the table again.

"Want a bite of my pizza?" Dion offered.

"No, I'm good, thanks," I said. "I have lots of grapes, that's all. Help yourself."

And that's exactly what he did. I liked that he felt comfortable enough with us to do that.

"So, Dion," Tori asked, "you gonna try out for the talent show?"

"Nope," he said.

"Are you afraid or is it because you don't think you have a talent?"

Dion took a drink of milk before he said, "I've got some pretty good moves, I guess. My little brother and I make up dance routines sometimes." He looked around before he leaned in and whispered, "Probably shouldn't have said that so loud."

"I don't get it. What's wrong with dancing?" I asked.

"Some people think it's . . . girly," he said.

Both Tori and I said the same thing at the exact same time. "What?"

I about choked on the grape in my mouth. "Haven't they seen *So You Think You Can Dance*? My mom and I love that show."

Dion said, "Well, you know, if it's not a sport, then it's not cool or whatever."

"My grandpa loves to dance," I said. "I mean, lots of guys love to dance, don't they?"

"Yes," Dion agreed. "They do. And I would love to join the dance program after school when soccer is over but . . ."

"But what?" Tori asked.

"There's not a single boy in it," he said softly.

"Maybe you should do it anyway," I suggested. "I mean, if it makes you happy."

"But if people are gonna make fun of him," Tori said, "that'd be tough. He already feels like he doesn't fit in, so it might only make things worse."

I didn't like how this conversation was going. "So it's better to pretend we're something we're not, just so people like us? Tori, that's kinda messed up, don't you think?"

Dion had been concentrating on curling the corners of his napkin. He looked uncomfortable and it made me feel so bad for him.

"There's this thing I do when I'm dancing that gives me confidence," he said before Tori could reply to me. "I wish I could do it with everything."

"What is it?" I asked, truly curious.

"When I'm dancing, I tell myself I'm not Dion. I pretend I'm someone else. Someone like Sammy Davis Jr. or Fred Astaire."

"Who are they?" Tori asked.

He looked shocked that she didn't know. I didn't know, either. "Couple of the most famous dancers of all time," he explained. "You've seriously never heard of Fred and Ginger?"

We both shook are heads.

He clucked his tongue. "They are unbelievable on the

dance floor. My mama has all their old movies on DVD. She sure does love 'em."

"So how does pretending to be Fred or Sammy help you?" I asked.

"If I'm someone like that, there's no way I can flop, right?" he said. "'Cause Sammy, man, he's got the moves, so if I'm him, then *I've* got the moves. You get me? It sort of tricks my brain or something."

"Okay," Tori said, smiling, "so you can be Sammy or Fred at the talent show. I want to see that! And you know what? If you impress people with your moves at the talent show, maybe they'll be more supportive of you doing dance after school."

"Or they'll laugh at me," Dion said.

"That's what I said," I told him. "Tori doesn't believe me."

"You really think they're going to magically change for one night?" Dion asked.

"The jerks probably won't even come to the talent show," she said. "Why would they? They don't like that kind of thing, do they?"

"I honestly don't know what they like," Dion replied. "But what I want to know is why."

"Why, what?" I asked.

"Why they gotta be that way?" he said. "If I ever acted that way at home, my dad would ground my butt for weeks. No more soccer. No more video games. Nothing. Just me and a long list of chores every day."

I thought of Ben. His moms are amazing. They never let their kids act mean toward them or anyone else. And I'd heard them lecture Tori and Ben about treating others with respect and what that looked like. Maybe sometimes parents were the reason kids acted badly, but it couldn't be the only reason.

I wished I could ask Ben why he'd done it. Why he'd started the notebook. Had he wanted to become more popular? Was it a way to look "cool" to the other boys at school? Or maybe he just thought it'd be something fun to do and was super clueless about it all?

I didn't have the answer, but I was really curious.

"I think people will be nice at the talent show, though," Tori said. "Especially if we bake all the mean boys cupcakes, like Hazel wants to do."

"You want to do what?" Dion asked.

I shrugged. "I don't know. It was just an idea. I mean, what else are we supposed to do? Maybe they don't have many people being nice to them, you know?"

"That's a sad thought," Dion said.

"Even if we don't hand out cupcakes," Tori said, "I think it'll be fine. It takes a lot for people to get up onstage and put themselves out there. I bet everyone will be their best selves."

Dion stared at her with his mouth open for a moment before he said, "You got a real hopeful heart, don't you? That's what my mama likes to say, that there are some people who have hopeful hearts and believe everything will turn out fine, no matter what other people think."

It made Tori sit up straight. "I like that. A hopeful heart."

"What does she call someone who doesn't have that?" I asked Dion.

"A negative Nelly," he said as he sort of rolled his eyes. "Whatever that means. How is it negative if you're saying things are bad when they're really and truly bad?"

I started writing words on my piece of paper while they kept talking.

> When it rains for weeks,
> it's hard to trust that someday
> sunshine will return.

After I finished, Dion leaned over and read it. When his eyes met mine, he smiled and said, "Hazel, that is something special. How do you do that? Hey, you know what? Maybe you should write haiku for the talent show."

It made me laugh. "I'd be booed off the stage after ten seconds. Who wants to watch someone write something? I might as well bring a plant onstage and say, 'Okay, we're all going to watch this plant grow, isn't that exciting?'"

Dion laughed, but Tori's face lit up like a lantern. "Wait. What if you *read* some of the haiku you've already written?"

I took a couple of grapes and popped them in my mouth. "My haiku are mine. I'm not sharing them with anyone."

Tori looked confused. "But you put them in books for people to find."

I wiggled my eyebrows. "Except no one knows I'm the one who wrote them. I'm, like, a haiku ninja."

Dion smiled. "Cool. I've never been friends with a ninja before."

"Lucky us," Tori teased.

He lifted his milk carton and said, "To friends."

I grabbed my can of cherry bubbly, and Tori picked up her water bottle. "Cheers," I said as we clinked our drinks.

"Cheers!" they said.

I was thrilled to have a new friend. But there was one thing I needed to do that I hadn't done yet. As soon as I got home, I needed to do it and get it over with.

I needed to find out if Dion was a part of the notebook.

CHAPTER NINETEEN

I searched for the initials *D.W.* as soon as I got home after soccer practice. Lucky for me, I didn't find them on a single page. Of course, even if I had found them, they could have belonged to someone besides Dion. But I was glad I didn't have to worry about it.

I thought back to third grade when a boy in our class, Jonathon, had wanted to be friends with Tori and me. At recess, he'd chased us with a handful of bark chips he'd scooped up from beneath the slide. Then he'd threatened to drop them down our shirts if we didn't play with him.

"What do you want to play?" Tori had asked.

"Why are you even asking?" I'd whispered in her ear. "I don't like him."

"Let's play tag," he'd said.

I'd looked over by the swings where a group of kids were running around. "Why don't you play with them?"

"They won't let me." He'd raised his hands full of bark chips and marched toward us. "But you will, right?"

I could still remember how helpless I'd felt. Play with

the mean kid or get a shirt full of bark chips. Those were not good choices. But we had to make one.

I was just about ready to say, "Fine, we'll play tag with you," but Tori had stepped forward and said, "Go ahead. Put those bark chips down my shirt. I don't care."

"Yeah you do," he'd said. "You'll get so many slivers. And who's going to pick them out for you, huh?"

"Go ahead," she'd said louder this time. "Do it! I'll scream and cry and you know what'll happen? You'll get sent to the principal's office while we're in PE class. That sounds fun, huh?"

I couldn't believe it. I couldn't believe what my friend had just done. Now Jonathon was the one with the hard choice. It was all on him. And you know what he did? He turned around, dropped the bark chips, and stomped off.

I nicknamed Tori "Genius" and that's all I called her for at least a month after that, until she told me she'd had enough and would like to go back to her normal name, thank you very much.

It felt a little bit like all the boys who'd written in the notebook had handfuls of bark chips they wanted to put down our shirts. It felt . . . cruel. If Dion had been a part of the notebook, I would have been so upset. But would I have decided I couldn't be friends with him? I don't know. I really liked him. I'd liked Ben once upon a time, too, though, and now? Not so much.

The thing is, I know people make mistakes. Especially

us kids. But passing around a notebook all about how girls look and mentioning specific body parts was so disgusting. And wrong. How could anyone not get that? How could anyone think, "Oh, this is fun," without thinking about how mean it was toward girls?

Mom called from the hallway, "Hazel, will you come to the store with me, please? I want you to pick out some cereal and some other things."

I stuffed the notebook under my pillow and hopped off my bed. "Okay. Coming!"

Pip was snacking on some veggies I'd shared with him. I always came home starving after practice, so Mom had a PB&J and some carrots and celery ready for me. No peanut butter for turtles, sadly, but he seemed to be completely happy with the carrots and celery. I gave his shell a little pat before I bounded out of my room and into the hallway.

"You working on homework already?" Mom asked.

"Uh, no. Reading a book."

She smiled. "Is it a good one?"

"Not really. I don't like how the girls are treated."

Mom cringed. "Uh-oh. That doesn't sound good."

No kidding.

In the produce aisle, we ran into my fifth-grade teacher, Ms. Lennon. Her brown hair was a little shorter, but other than that, she looked exactly the same. I was so happy to see her, I held my arms out for a hug without thinking about whether she'd like it or not. I didn't have to worry; she wrapped her arms around me, and it was the best hug I'd had in a long time.

"It's so good to see you, Hazel," she said. "How's middle school?"

"Um . . . well, I miss fifth grade a lot."

"I miss you, too. Read any good books lately?"

I spoke fast so my mom wouldn't get a chance to mention the book I'd told her about earlier. The one that didn't treat girls very well. Can you imagine my mom mentioning it in front of my teacher and then one of them asking for the title? I don't know what I would have done.

"There's one book I'm really loving right now," I said. "It's called *Front Desk*. Have you heard of it?"

"Yes!" she said. "I loved it, too. So many wonderful books coming out lately, aren't there? You know, one you might love is called *Up for Air* by Laurie Morrison. It's perfect for middle schoolers."

This was one of the things I loved about Ms. Lennon— she read the same books her students did.

"Thanks! I'll check it out. Sometimes I like to read while Pip, my tortoise, is out of his box, exploring."

"You have a tortoise?" she asked.

"Well, kind of," I said, not sure how to explain it all. "He was left in a box in the parking lot of Ruby's. I've been trying to find a new home for him but it's hard. They live a long time and I'm just not sure . . ."

I stopped and stared at Ms. Lennon. She was my favorite teacher so far. The one who made me fall in love with writing haiku. The one who didn't believe in worksheets for homework because reading books is way more important. The one who told me middle school might be challenging sometimes, for different reasons, but I was kind and capable and everything would be okay, eventually.

"I just had an idea," I said. "What if you took Pip as a class pet? All the kids could help take care of him. They'd love that, wouldn't they? I mean, *I* would have loved that."

Ms. Lennon bit her lip like she was thinking hard. After a moment she said, "I have to be honest. I don't know much about tortoises. Do they require a lot of care?"

"Not really," I said. "Just have to make sure he stays warm and has fresh fruit and veggies to eat. Oh, and you'd have to clean his house pretty often. But the students could help, couldn't they?"

"Yes," she said. "They certainly could. It's early in the year and I'm already having some trouble with bullying. A class pet may be just the thing to help with that." She pulled a pen and pad of paper out of her purse. "Can you give me your number, Hazel? Let me take a couple of days to think about it and I'll give you a call, okay? I want to check with some of the other teachers and see what they have say. I've never had a class pet before, so I need to make sure I'm not getting into something I can't handle."

I wrote my number down for her, and she tucked the paper into her purse.

"Thank you for considering it," my mom said. "This is really exciting."

"You're welcome," Ms. Lennon said. "Talk to you in a couple of days, Hazel."

As Mom rolled the cart toward the cereal aisle, she said, "Great thinking, Hazel. I'm so proud of you."

With anyone else, I might have been too scared to ask. But it hadn't been hard asking Ms. Lennon.

Even if she hadn't been interested, I knew she would have been nice about it. That's what seemed so scary to me when wanting to speak up about something—not knowing what the response would be. People can say the most hurtful things.

Using my voice would be a lot easier if I didn't have to worry about whether or not it's safe for me to do that.

CHAPTER TWENTY

I went to school early the next day to see if I could get the book Ms. Lennon had recommended since I was almost finished with my other one. But as I walked toward the library, I found Dion up against the lockers with Preston and Aaron, who were yelling mean things at him.

I felt the hairs on my arms stand straight up. I looked around, hoping I'd see a teacher. But no one else was around right then. Only me. I had to do something. I just had to.

"Hey, Dion, there you are, I was looking for you. Come on, the librarian is waiting for us. She has those books we were asking about, remember?"

Preston and Aaron stopped, turned around, and looked at me. Then they turned back to Dion. "Wait. You're friends with Camel Lips?" Preston asked. "Well, that explains a lot."

I walked over, said, "Excuse me," and pushed myself between Aaron and Preston, catching a whiff of BO as I reached for Dion's hand. "Come on. Let's go."

I did it really fast and I think they were so surprised, they didn't know what to say or do. Dion squeezed my hand tight as we hurried down the hall toward the library.

Once we got inside, Dion crumpled into a chair and put his arms and head down on the table. He was trying not to make a sound as he cried.

I sat down beside him, wishing I knew the perfect thing to say to make him feel better. It was another superpower of my mom's that I longed for.

Mrs. Thompson looked at us from across the room where she was shelving books. "Everything okay?" she called out.

"Yeah, um . . . his allergies are really bad today," I told her.

She went back to her work and I pulled out my phone and texted Tori.

Come to the library when you get here.
Dion's upset.

I went to Mrs. Thompson's desk and grabbed a few tissues and took them back to Dion. After I handed them to him, he wiped at his face. "Sorry," he said softly.

"What for? You didn't do anything wrong."

"For crying again. I'm such a baby."

"You're not a baby." I sat down and scooted my chair closer to his. "When something hurts, we cry. My dad says that's what makes us human. You're just human, Dion. That's all."

He sniffled as he said, "I wish I was *super*human. Wish I could disappear whenever I wanted. Or fly. Or something."

"Me too." I replied. "Believe me. Me too."

"You got a haiku about that?" he asked with half a smile.

"Maybe you should try writing one. Writing takes your mind off other things, you know?"

"Maybe I will," he said. He picked at his thumbnail for a moment before he looked up at me. "Thanks, Hazel. I don't know what I would have done if you hadn't come by right then. It was really brave of you."

I didn't know how to respond to that, so I simply said, "You're welcome."

A few minutes later, Tori came rushing in. "What is it? What happened?"

"Not what, who," I said. "Preston and Aaron."

Her eyes narrowed and she clenched her fists. "I'm so sick of them. We need to do something."

"Nothing we can do," Dion said. "They'd just say I was lying."

"Next time, you should try and get video of it," Tori said. "We need proof."

"If I pulled out my phone, they'd take it," Dion said. "Bet I'd never see it again."

Tori's face drooped. "Oh. You're probably right."

Other kids started walking in. It didn't seem like this was something we could keep talking about with other people around.

"We should probably go," Dion said. "Get ready for class and stuff."

"It's not fair," Tori whispered. "It's not fair that we have to deal with this every day. Do we really have to live like this for the next three years?"

Dion and I didn't answer her. All I could think about was what she'd said earlier. *We need proof.*

I had proof that our school had issues. Big issues. But it probably wasn't the kind of proof Tori had been imagining. Still, maybe if I could just get brave enough to tell them about it, they could help me figure out what to do with it.

Tell them, I thought. *Now's your chance.*

"Um," I said.

They both turned and looked at me.

"What?" Tori said. "What is it?"

I stood up. "You guys go on without me. I don't want you to be late. I have to see if they have a book I really want to read."

They said okay as they got up and walked toward the door. Dion thought I was brave, but right then, that didn't seem true to me. Not at all.

Later, in band class, I found another note on the music stand where I sit. I looked around to see if I could figure out who had left it, but there were a bunch of people in there already.

I opened the note and read it.

You know your new boyfriend is a fairy, right?

It made me so mad, I crumpled the piece of paper into a tiny ball. As I threw it into the trash, I stared at Aaron, who was also in my class. He played the trumpet. While I stared, he shrugged his shoulders as if to say, "Who, me?" It had to be him who'd written the note. It just had to be. But I had no way to prove it. Unless . . .

I turned around and went back to the little trash can that sat next to the door. There were mostly just papers in there—tardy slips, doodles, and whatnot. The little ball I wadded up was sitting there, right on top. I reached in and grabbed it. As soon as I did, Aaron yelled, "Ew!" from across the room. "Why are you digging in the trash, Hazel?"

Everyone, and I mean everyone, stopped what they were doing. A hundred eyes were on me. I wanted to crawl into that tiny trash can and never come out again. I couldn't decide if I should defend myself or stay quiet or what. Fortunately, our band teacher, Mr. Bailey, came to my rescue. "Aaron, mind your own business, please. And everyone, let's get organized; the bell is going to ring any second."

People started chattering again and I went to my seat, the crumpled note held tightly in my hand. When no one was looking, I stuffed it into the pocket of my jeans. After school, I planned to look and see if any of the handwriting in the notebook matched the note.

Who knew the notebook would end up being so helpful, in a roundabout way?

CHAPTER TWENTY-ONE

I found Aaron's initials, A. A. for Aaron Adams, throughout the notebook. On my page, he was the one who'd written "Literally the worst." On other pages, he'd written things like, "Such a dog" and "So ugly, I bet her brother wouldn't even kiss her."

And, just as I'd suspected, his handwriting matched the writing on the note. It made me so mad. Like, why me? Why did he decide to pick on me? What had I ever done to him? Nothing. I was new to the school. New to band. I was a sixth-grade girl who was so shy, I hardly ever spoke to anyone in that class. It really didn't make sense why he'd chosen me.

I was pretty sure I'd found Preston's initials and comments, too. No surprise, these boys who were mean to people at school every day were also mean to girls in writing. I grabbed one of my journals and wrote a haiku.

When dark clouds appear,
take them as a strict warning—
the rain is coming.

With all that out of the way, I set the notebooks down and jumped off my bed with a loud *thump*. It shook the whole room and made me laugh. I'd gone right upstairs when I'd come home, so now I needed to go back to the kitchen for Pip's afternoon snack. But when I went to check on him, I saw something I hadn't seen since I'd brought him home. He'd tucked his legs and head in so all I could see was the shell.

"What's going on?" I asked him, kneeling down and petting his shell as I did. "Oh no, did I scare you?"

Obviously, he didn't answer me. He didn't do anything. It was so strange to see his shell like that. It almost seemed like he was . . . dead. No head. No stumpy tail. No cute little turtle feet. It was so sad!

"Pip?" I said. I leaned closer and I could see his little beady eyes inside the shell.

"Pip, please don't be scared. I'm sorry if you thought I was a big animal coming to eat you. I'd never eat you! And I'm not a large animal, even if sometimes I think being an elephant would be much better than being a human."

How long did a tortoise stay hidden when they were scared? I wondered.

I leaned back and waited. As I sat there, watching him, this strange feeling washed over me. It was like I was watching . . . myself. Shy. Afraid. Hidden in my shell most of the time.

Was that how I really wanted to be? Afraid of

everything? Afraid to do *anything*? Just a shell of a person, walking around, angry about how things are but not doing anything about it?

"Please come out, Pip," I said softly as I gently stroked his shell. "Please? I'm so sorry. I really am."

That's when I started to cry. I didn't want to. I didn't even know *why* I was crying. It wasn't because Pip was hiding. He'd come out eventually, I knew. But I wanted things to be different. So many things felt wrong, and I didn't know what to do about any of it.

Mostly, I felt alone. It felt like I was on a deserted island all by myself and I had no idea how to hunt or fish to keep myself alive. Other people could probably figure it out, but me? I probably wouldn't even pick any berries to eat because I'd be too scared that they might be poisonous. No, better to starve to death than take a small chance that I might eat poisonous berries.

That's when my tears turned into laughter. Because it was all completely ridiculous. Things weren't *that* bad. I wasn't on a deserted island with nothing to eat. I had a home, I had friends, I had a family. Just because I had a stupid notebook I didn't know what to do with didn't mean it was the end of the world.

For a minute, I thought about telling my parents. But what if they went straight to the principal? He seemed to be very much on the side of boys, not girls. He probably wouldn't see anything wrong with the notebook. And what if he made me do something to punish me, in a roundabout sort of way? He could put me on the stage at the next assembly and make me talk about what I'd found. Not only would I vomit if I had to do that, half the school would hate me.

"I don't know what to do," I whispered to Pip. After sitting there for a couple more minutes, I decided that maybe right now wasn't the time to worry about me. I took a deep breath and got to my feet.

"I'm going to get you some food. Maybe that will get you back to normal."

I went to the bathroom and washed my face before I headed to the kitchen. If only I had a sister or brother to talk to about all this, I thought. Sometimes being an only child is really, really lonely.

Because one of my mom's superpowers is looking at me for half a second and knowing when I'm unhappy, I knew she'd say something. And that's exactly what happened.

"Hazel, are you okay?" she asked. "Did something happen at school?"

"I'm fine," I said. "I jumped off my bed and scared Pip, so I feel bad. That's all."

"Is he hiding in his shell?" she asked me.

"Yes. It's so weird seeing him like that. I don't like it."

"It's natural for them, though," she said. "Gosh, wouldn't it be nice if we could tuck ourselves into a shell and take a little quiet break whenever we needed one?"

"If I could do that, I'd probably never come out." I was kind of teasing, but I also sort of thought that was true.

As I reached into the fridge for some cabbage and grapes for Pip, Mom said, "It makes me so sad to hear you say that, Hazel."

"Sorry," I said when I turned around. I set the bags on the counter. "I'm sorry I'm not like you. I wish for that sometimes, you know."

She came over and pulled me into a hug. "Oh, honey, you don't need to apologize. You are who you are, and I love you so much." She kissed the top of my head and then said, "But you know what I wish? I wish I could help you believe you are on equal footing as everyone else and that you should stand proud."

I kind of groaned. "Equal footing? You mean, like, how boys do mean things and people tell them, 'Well, boys will be boys'? Or how us girls have to watch how we dress because it's not good for the boys? Or how you didn't get a promotion because some guy got it instead?"

She didn't say anything for a moment. Then, she did something I hadn't expected. At all. She pumped her fist in the air. "Hazel! Did you just hear yourself? That was amazing! You spoke up and out, and oh my gosh, I'm *so* proud of you!"

"You are?"

She grabbed my hands and squeezed them tightly. "Yes!

Don't you see? You've had it in you this whole time! Did you feel it?"

"Feel what?" I asked.

"The power you had as you spoke your mind?"

"But it was only you and me," I said. "I knew you'd love me no matter what. With other people . . ."

"It's more frightening," she said, nodding. "I know. I get it. And if you don't feel safe for some reason, then by all means, you don't have to say a word if you don't want to. About anything. But if there are people around you who have your back, remember this moment, okay? You can do it. You spoke *so* well, Hazel."

"Thanks. I guess."

It was hard to be excited about something that kind of terrified me. I grabbed Pip's food and headed back to my room.

"Pip!" I said when I saw that he'd come out of his shell. "I'm so happy to see you."

As I placed his snack in the box beside him, I realized it was basically the same thing my mom had said to me. I'd come out of my shell. Only for a minute, but I'd done it. And maybe, just maybe, that meant I could do it again.

CHAPTER TWENTY-TWO

As I walked down the hall Friday morning toward my locker, I saw girls standing by the talent show sign-up sheet, taking selfies. They really seemed to have the selfie thing down. I couldn't turn away as I watched how they positioned themselves a certain way, made sure their hair hung just right across the front of one shoulder, and tilted their heads just slightly.

This was the popular crowd Tori wanted to be a part of. She thought it was ridiculous that I wasn't allowed to take selfies. She wasn't mean about it or anything. She was actually thoughtful and hardly took them when I was around because she didn't want me to feel bad. But I knew she was allowed to take them and post them to her private Instagram account. It was a world I wasn't a part of, and it didn't take much to remind me of that. Would she comment on these girls' photos later? Would she tell them how cute they looked? Tell them how excited she was to see their performance at the talent show? Would they comment back?

I was wondering all this when who should walk up but Tori herself, in an adorable pink-and-black polka-dot button-up blouse. She hadn't seen me, so I just stood back and watched as she waited her turn for the sign-up sheet. After she'd added her name, the girls encouraged her to take a selfie, too. She smoothed down her long, blonde hair, held the phone out, and smiled.

With that out of the way, they started chatting and giggling, and I felt so left out I almost wanted to run over there and tell her I'd changed my mind, that I did want to do the talent show with her, after all.

But not really. What did I know about dancing or sign language or anything like that? Not a thing.

"Hey," Dion said from behind me, startling me so much I jumped a little.

"Oh, hi," I said.

"What are you doing?" he asked.

"Watching a bunch of popular girls sign up for the talent show," I told him.

"You want to do something?" he asked. "You can, you know. Doesn't matter if you're popular or not."

"You sure about that?"

He smiled. "No."

Just then, Tori noticed us. "Hey!" she said as she scurried over to us. "Do you want me to add your name, Hazel? So you can sign and dance alongside me?"

"Wow, that sounds awesome," Dion said. "You should do it."

"I don't think so," I said. "I wouldn't—"

Tori stuck her bottom lip out. "But you haven't even heard the song that I'm going to do. The song is everything, isn't it, Dion?"

"I mean, whether you can actually sing is probably the most important thing," Dion said nicely. "But after that, yeah, the song is definitely up there."

She leaned in and whispered the name of the song so only Dion and I could hear.

"You really doing that?" Dion asked.

With determination and confidence in her voice, she said, "Yes. I am."

And then Dion did something I wouldn't have guessed in a hundred years. "We should both do it, Hazel."

"What?" Both Tori and I said, staring at our friend as if he'd just told us he had an entire chocolate cake in his backpack.

He gave us a half grin. "You said I should do the talent show to prove I'm a good dancer. Well, I'd rather do it with you two than anyone else, or, even worse, by myself."

"I love it!" Tori said. "Oh my gosh, this is the best idea ever. Ben is doing something with some of his friends, so we can show him we're just as good, if not better!" She looked at me. "What do you say?"

My stomach lurched. "You guys . . ."

"Come on, Hazel," Tori said. "It'll be fun. We'll be with you every step of the way, right, Dion?"

"Literally, every step," he said.

"I don't know," I said. "I'm sorry, I just don't think . . ."

"Here's what I'm going to do," Tori said. "I'm going to sign us all up. You can try, right? And if you can't, then you can't. But maybe you can and then we're all signed up and ready to go. Okay?"

I felt dizzy. "Yeah. Okay."

Tori jumped up and down for a second and then ran back over to the sign-up sheet to add our names with hers.

Dion looked at me. "You're not just doing it for me, are you? Because, Hazel, if you really don't want to, you don't have to. I'd never want to make you do anything you don't want to do."

He was right. I had said yes mostly for him. Because I didn't want him to be afraid anymore of doing what he loved to do. If he could get up on that stage and dance, going to a dance class after school might not be such a big deal. And hopefully he could prove to everyone that he had a reason for going to dance class—because he was an amazing dancer.

"It's okay," I said. "I need to try, just like she said."

He held out his fist so I bumped it with mine. "You're a good egg, Hazel. One of my grandma's favorite things to say, right there. You two should come to my house and practice. You can meet Grandma Dorothy. I think you'd like her a lot."

"I'd love that," I told him.

"Love what?" Tori said.

Dion told her what he'd told me and she was all for it. "How about next Friday afternoon?" he asked. "Teacher in-service day, right? How about three o'clock?"

"Sounds good," Tori said.

We started walking toward our locker. Tori said, "Okay, with that out of the way for now, we need to start planning for Halloween, which is coming up a lot sooner than mid-December. Like, a couple weeks. I was thinking we could dress up as the three blind mice from the nursery rhyme. Wouldn't that be fun?"

I was beginning to wonder if my best friend never slept. She probably stayed up to scheme, plot, and plan how to be the most clever, fun, talented person in middle school.

"I have to say, that is genius." I smiled at her. "Genius."

She groaned. "No, not that nickname again! But if you like the idea, Mimi said she'd love to help us. She's good with costumes, right, Hazel?"

Last year she'd helped Tori and I make two long, comfy shirts for our costumes, one that said NETFLIX and one that said CHILL. Everyone who saw us thought it was the cutest thing.

"You guys," Dion said, "what if I hate mice? Like, really, really hate them?"

"Why?" I asked. "They're just little rodents with cute ears. They don't hurt anyone."

Dion kind of grimaced. "That's not exactly true. See,

we were at the grocery store one time and my little brother had to pee really bad. So my mama asked me to take him back to the restroom. Well, you had to go through these double doors into this big storage-type room and there was a mouse sitting there and before I could stop him, Kalen bent down to pet the mouse and it latched onto his finger."

"Oh no," Tori said. "It bit him?"

"Yep. Swelled up so bad, he had to go to the doctor and get a shot and stuff. Oh, but that's not the best part. The best part was that he'd flicked his finger in the air to get the mouse off and it'd flown across the room. Well, a bunch of the workers at the store had to try and find the thing because they wanted to check and see if it had rabies."

"Did they find it?" I asked.

"Yeah, it was dead. They think it ate some poison and was half dead when we found it. That's why it didn't run away when it saw us. Anyway, you can see why I don't like mice, right?"

"But we'll be cute mice," Tori said.

"That don't bite," I added.

He held his hands up, like he was surrendering. "Okay, okay, mice it is."

"We have a lot to look forward to, don't we?" Tori said cheerily.

Right, there was plenty to look forward to—a talent

show I wasn't talented enough for, a notebook I didn't know what to do with, and a tortoise that would probably be leaving me. I wished I could feel happy like Tori, but even with a fun Halloween costume, what I mostly felt was worried.

CHAPTER TWENTY-THREE

Saturday morning, before our soccer game, Ms. Lennon called me. "Hazel, I hope you're going to be happy to know that I've decided to take your tortoise!"

Tears filled my eyes and I wasn't sure if they were happy tears or sad. A little bit of both, I guess. There was no one I trusted more than Ms. Lennon. But I would miss him so, so much.

"Really?" I managed. "You're sure?"

"Yes, I'm sure. The other teachers assured me it won't be hard and between all of us, we believe we can give Pip a good home for many years to come."

"Thank you so much, Ms. Lennon."

"Well, thank you for trusting me with him. Now, I'm wondering if it might be possible for you to bring him to the school Monday morning? I'm going to get everything he needs this weekend, so I'll be ready. And since middle school starts an hour later than the elementary school, I thought first thing in the morning might work the best?"

"Okay. I think my dad can bring me," I said. "He usually works from home on Mondays."

"Wonderful. I'll see you then. Thanks, Hazel. Goodbye."

"Bye."

I rushed out of my room to tell my parents, who were at the kitchen table, drinking coffee and reading the paper. The kitchen smelled good, like cinnamon. Mom was probably baking muffins or banana bread.

They were thrilled with the news, and Dad said he'd be happy to take me to deliver the class's new pet Monday morning.

"I hope she's reading everything she can about tortoises," I said as I sat at the table.

"I'm sure she is," Mom said. "She's smart and compassionate, which means she'll want to do the best she can for Pip."

"Do you think she'll keep his name?" I asked.

"I don't see why not," Dad said.

"Maybe she'll want the kids to name him," I said.

Mom shook her head. "The problem with that is she'd have twenty-five different opinions and every child would think their idea was the best. It's much easier to keep the one he has now, right?"

I shrugged. "Maybe. I hope so. I can't imagine calling him something else. She won't mind if I visit him once in a while, will she?"

Mom got up and went to the oven as the timer went off. "I'm sure she'd love that, Hazel."

I watched as she pulled the pan out of the oven.

"Banana bread?" I asked.

"Yep," she said. "Need to let it cool for a few minutes, then I'll cut into it."

"I'm glad he'll have a good home," I told them. "But it's going to be hard to say goodbye."

And what if I couldn't do it? What if I got there and giving Pip up was just too hard? I mean, every day when I came home, no matter how bad of a day it was, he was there, ready to sit with me and listen to what I had to say. I was going to miss that. A lot.

"Don't think of it as goodbye," Dad said with a smile. "Think of it as sending him on vacation. A nice vacation where he'll meet lots of people who are going to make sure he has the best life possible."

"They better be good to him," I said. "Ms. Lennon said she has a bullying problem. I don't want them to pick on poor Pip."

"She's trying to teach them to look beyond themselves, I think," Mom said. "That's a good lesson, for sure."

"But what if some of the kids don't want to learn that lesson?" I asked.

"They're not going to hurt a helpless tortoise," Dad said.

I wanted to tell him that lots of kids are helpless, too, but that doesn't stop the bullying. Except if I said that, they'd probably think I was talking about myself and get really worried. I didn't want that.

"I hope so" is all I said as I stood up. "I'm gonna go get ready. Can I have some bread in the car, Mom?"

"Yes," she said. "But not too much. Don't want you to get sick." She got up and reached for my water bottle on the counter. "And here. Hydrate!"

I took a long drink. "Happy?"

She broke out in a silly dance as she sang, "So happy. So happy. Hydration makes me happy!"

"Good one, Mom. Maybe you should perform in our school's talent show in December."

Her eyes got big. "Ooh, fun! I love talent shows. Are you . . . ?" Her voice trailed off. "Never mind. Go get ready so we can head out."

"Actually, I am," I said. "My new friend, Dion, and I agreed to sign the song that Tori's going to sing. And probably dance a little, too. I don't know, maybe I'll chicken out, but for now, that's the plan."

Mom came over and gave me a hug. "So proud of you. And that's all I'm going to say. Go get ready."

When we got to the field, my teammates were warming up. I threw my bag on the ground next to my parents, who were setting up chairs with all the other grown-ups.

"Have a good game, Hazel!" I heard Jeanie yell.

I waved as I ran out to join my team. From the other side of the field, away from all the parents, I heard a familiar voice yell, "You going to try stealing the ball today, Hazel? 'Cause you're good at that, right? Stealing?"

I didn't turn around. I knew it was Ben, and I knew he wanted to rattle me. I had to try my best to ignore him.

Except I couldn't. I knew he was watching me. I knew he was ready to pounce again when he had the chance. He'd try to get me to admit I took the notebook. How much longer could I pretend that I didn't? How much longer could I act like everything was fine when everything was *not* fine?

When the game started, we got the ball right away and one of our best players, Monique, passed it to me and I took it down the field and tried to pass it to Tori, but an opponent stole it from me and took off with it. I glanced over at Ben. He was smiling.

We lost the game, and I was furious. The soccer field has always felt like a second home to me—a place where I could just be myself and get lost in the game. Usually, everything else in the world faded away except for me and the ball and the players on the field. But not today.

I went straight home to spend every minute I could with Pip. I took about a hundred pictures over the weekend and practically cried with every one. Did he even realize how much he'd helped me?

He'd shown me that curling up into a shell and being afraid all the time was no way to live. It was because of him that I'd decided to get the notebook away from Ben. Even if I had no idea what to do with it now, I was proud of the fact that I'd done it. And it was all thanks to Pip.

As I cried next to his box Sunday night, I asked, "Even if you don't live with me, we can be friends for the next seventy or eighty years, can't we?"

Like always, he just stared at me. But I swear his little mouth curved up into a smile, ever so slightly.

CHAPTER TWENTY-FOUR

Monday morning, Dad helped me carry the box to the car. After we got in, he said, "You okay?"

"I think so," I said. "I hope I don't cry in front of everyone."

"It's okay to cry," he said as he backed out of the driveway. "They'll understand."

"Dad, I wish, but that's not how it works."

"How do you know?" he asks. "Do you cry a lot at school?"

I almost said, "No, but only because I tell myself not to." Instead I just said, "No. But people aren't always as nice as you think."

"When I was fifteen," he said, "I was in a band with a few friends and a lady hired us to play at her daughter's sweet sixteen party. We'd put flyers around town and she'd seen one of them and thought it'd be fun to have a real band for the party. So we got up there on the little makeshift stage and, Hazel, I was so nervous, I vomited. Right there. In front of everyone. And if that wasn't bad enough, I started crying after that."

"Whoa," I said. "That sounds . . . horrible."

"It really was. We'd never played in front of anyone before. We'd just practiced in a basement. We hadn't considered that maybe it would be nerve-racking to play for an audience."

"Were people mad?" I asked. "Like, the lady who hired you—what did she say?"

He stopped at a light. Little kids were walking to school. I felt a pain in my chest because I wished that were still me.

"That's what I wanted to tell you," he said. "Everyone was so incredibly kind about it. They got the stage cleaned up, got me some ginger ale, and thirty minutes later, my friends and I were back on that stage, playing our hearts out. It'll be okay, Hazel. There are good people in the world. Please, never forget that."

I looked out the window and tried really hard not to roll my eyes. Why can't parents understand that sometimes you just need them to say, "I'm sorry you're feeling that way," and then stop?

He parked the car and then took the box out of the back seat. We walked into the school along with some kids. The cafeteria was right by the front doors, so the scents of sausages and cinnamon rolls drifted out to greet us. My heart ached as we walked down the hall. It felt so familiar but also a little bit strange. I didn't belong here anymore, no matter how much I wished I did. I was a sixth grader now. Middle school was supposed to be my place, but it felt like I'd never love it even half as much as I'd loved Hoover.

On the last day of fifth grade, Ms. Lennon had called us up to her desk, one by one, to give us a book she'd picked out for each of us. She'd given me the book *The Poet's Dog*, about an Irish wolfhound who lives in the woods and can talk, but only children and poets can understand him.

"Since you're now a poet, I think you'll love this book," she'd told me. "I know it's short and doesn't look like much, but trust me, it's a sweet, tender story, and I really hope you enjoy it as much as I did."

And I had. But even more than the story, I treasured the message Ms. Lennon had written on the inside cover:

Dear Hazel,
May you never forget the value that words have in our lives. And may you keep writing, because the world surely needs more of <u>your</u> words, especially.
Love,
Ms. Lennon

Sometimes I wished that I could have stayed in fifth grade forever. And I hated feeling that way. I wanted to be like Tori—excited about growing up and everything that came with it. That feeling had to hit me someday. Didn't it?

"Hazel, hi! Look, it's me!"

I looked down and saw my kindergarten buddy from last year. Our class would get together with his every couple of weeks and read books together. "Hey, River, how are you?"

"Good. Are coming back to this school?" He fiddled with one of the drawstrings on his sweatshirt. "Because I'm in a new room. I'm in first grade now!"

"I know," I said. "That's so exciting. I'm at the middle school now, but I came to see Ms. Lennon for a little bit. Are you reading lots of good books this year?"

His brown eyes sparkled as he said, "Yep! I can read a lot by myself now."

"Cool," I said as I put my hand out for a high five, which he happily gave me. "See you later, okay?"

He waved and said, "Okay, bye," as he turned and went into Mr. Knight's room. I peeked in and oh my gosh, the chairs and tables looked so tiny.

It was like Dad could read my mind. "Hard to believe you used to be that small, huh?"

"Yeah" was all I could manage. How ridiculous was it that I actually felt jealous of a first grader?

Dad continued walking and I followed. We turned down a second hallway. Ms. Lennon's room was the last one on the left.

Walking into that classroom felt like going home. But knowing I couldn't stay for long was like a punch in my stomach. I looked around and took everything in. The wall of books I used to love to explore. The haiku she'd written on the whiteboard. And the nice, new wooden home with a heat lamp on one end, all set up for Pip.

"Good morning, Hazel," Ms. Lennon said as she stood up from her desk. "So good to see you. And hello, Mr. Wallace. Thanks so much for doing this."

"Happy to do it," Dad said.

I took a deep breath and told myself to be strong. "His house looks amazing. Pip is going to love it."

"I have a smaller one at my place as well. That way I can take him home with me on the weekends." She went to the box still in my dad's hands and peered in. "Oh, isn't he a beauty. Wow. Hazel, would you like to stay and hear me introduce Pip to the students?"

I looked at Dad. "Is that all right?"

He nodded. "You bet."

Ms. Lennon got me a chair and set it by her desk. Dad put the box on the floor behind me, so the students wouldn't be able to see into it easily.

"The children are going to have a lot of questions when they come in, but I'm going to tell them to sit in their seats so I can share what's going on with everyone."

"Good plan," Dad said.

Ms. Lennon smiled. "We'll see if it works. Sometimes it's like herding cats, you know."

She went to the door and with every student, she greeted them and said she had a surprise she would share as soon as they were all in their seats. Everyone pointed or gasped at the sight of Pip's house. As they spoke to their classmates, they tried to guess what kind of animal might go in there. Some of the guesses I heard were snakes, frogs, hamsters, rats, and even a bearded dragon.

When the entire class was seated, Ms. Lennon stood up and said, "Good morning, everyone. This is Hazel Wallace. She was one of my students last year. And she's brought our class something really special. For the first time ever, this room is going to have a class pet."

The kids pumped their fists in the air and cheered. As I looked out at their faces, I could tell they were super excited.

Ms. Lennon looked at me and said, "Hazel, can you introduce us to Pip? Please stay in your seats until we're done. Then I'll give everyone a chance to say hello to our new friend."

I reached behind the chair and picked up Pip. Then I held him gently, extending my hands out a bit so everyone could see. "Pip is very happy to meet you," I said. And then came lots of comments.

"It's a turtle!"

"A tortoise, I think."

"He's so cute!"

"Why's he named Pip?"

Ms. Lennon let them chatter a little before she quieted them down again. Then she said, "Children, I'm sure I don't have to tell you that having a pet is a big responsibility. He'll rely on us to feed him, to keep his cage clean, and to show him love and kindness. Always. This is not my class pet, this is *our* class pet. Understand?"

Most of them nodded their heads while a couple shouted, "Yes!"

"I want you to imagine," Ms. Lennon said, "what it must be like for him to be here, in this new place, with a classroom full of children and not in a natural habitat." She stopped for a moment. "Do you think he might be a little scared?"

They nodded again.

"One of the most important things I can teach you this year is that every creature, human or otherwise, deserves to be treated with kindness, empathy, and respect. We've been talking about those words and what they mean, so I hope you remember. Pip is counting on us to be the very best humans we can be.

"See, the trouble with turtles is that the hard shell gives the illusion that they can't be hurt. But it's not true. In fact, their shells have nerve endings, so they can feel things. Sometimes we try to pretend that our actions or words won't hurt anyone, but of course they do. And I will not tolerate anyone treating our precious class pet with anything other than kindness. No poking his shell. No hitting his shell. Nothing but gentle hands all the time. Okay?"

As I sat there, holding Pip close to my heart, I thought about the jerks at my middle school. Every day, they did what Ms. Lennon was talking about—pretended that their actions or words didn't hurt others. But they did. They hurt a lot. And even worse? They got away with it over and over again.

"Thank you, Hazel, for trusting us with Pip," Ms. Lennon said. "I think he's going to teach us a lot of important lessons. Lessons we will remember the rest of our lives."

They weren't the only ones.

CHAPTER TWENTY-FIVE

I didn't cry until I got to the car. And then I cried a whole lot. Dad hugged me and didn't say a word, and for that, I was grateful.

"We need to get going," he finally said. "I don't want you to be late."

I nodded. "I know. Let's go. I'll be fine."

As he drove toward school, I texted Tori.

I just said goodbye to Pip and I'm so sad.

It took her a while to respond, which wasn't like her. Finally, my phone pinged.

Oh no. I'm so sorry. But you found him a good home, right? I have to go to the dentist this morning. Then Mom is taking me out to lunch afterward. Talk after school?

I texted a quick reply, then put my phone away. It'd be just me this morning. Would the tripping boys let me go, or would they be even worse since I'd be alone? I guess I was about to find out.

When Dad pulled up to the front doors, he said, "You're a good person, Hazel Wallace. I'm proud of you. I understand that you're sad, but with time, it'll get better. You'll see. Try and have a good day, okay? I'll pick you up since you don't have your bike."

"Yeah, I know. Bye, Dad."

"Bye, sweetheart."

Just my luck, Aaron and Preston were hanging out right inside the front doors.

"Well, look who's here," Preston said. "The girl who's hoping Ben will want to kiss her ugly camel lips."

There were kids all around. I wasn't really alone.

"Don't be stupid," Aaron said. "He's a loser. You can do better!"

"So, you like her or something?" Preston asked.

Aaron punched Preston's arm as he said, "No!"

Enough. I'd had enough. I glared at them and yelled, "Stop it!"

They both started laughing, which was so rude but not surprising.

I turned around and marched toward my locker, my heart beating fast. I told myself to never forget this feeling. I'd managed to say something. It'd only been two words, but they were two important words. And those words showed them that I wasn't afraid to stand up for myself.

Wasn't afraid to stick my neck out so I could move forward.

It'd felt scary for a few seconds, but now? It felt good.

At lunch, Dion came into the library with his bagged lunch from home and sat down next to me. A couple of girls were sitting together across the table from us, drawing pictures. And that was it for the library lunch crowd.

"No Tori today?" Dion asked.

"Dentist appointment," I explained as I opened my baggie of apple slices to share. "Lucky her, she doesn't have to listen to me whine about how hard it was to let Pip go this morning."

"Not really sure a dentist appointment is lucky," he said as he took out his sandwich. "But I'm sorry it was hard, Hazel. Probably just gonna be that way for a while. I know you love Pip. And he loves you. My mama always says we have to hold on to that love, 'cause it's always there, even if the one we love isn't, you know?"

"Yeah. You're right. Thank you."

That was a good friend. He didn't tell me everything would be okay. He didn't try to change the subject so he didn't have to deal with it. He just imagined how I probably felt and knew what I needed to hear.

"You're welcome," he said. Then he smiled. "You know, I'm glad I met you, Hazel. School doesn't suck quite as bad, thanks to you and Tori."

I laughed. "Hey, same!" And that's when I knew. I knew

that I finally had someone who I could tell about the notebook.

I glanced over at the girls. They seemed to be completely lost in their drawings. Still, I leaned in and lowered my voice to a whisper. "I need advice about something. But you have to promise you won't tell anyone unless I say it's okay. Like, if I tell you, it's just going to be the two of us that know about it for a while. So, do you think you can keep it a secret?"

"One hundred percent," he said. "Wait, you aren't even going to tell Tori?"

I shook my head. "No, because her brother is involved."

Now he looked worried. "Okay. Involved in what?"

"Well, I found something," I told him.

"Yeah?"

I took a deep breath and continued. "A notebook. I found a notebook with the names of lots of girls who go to this school. Boys are rating them and commenting on their looks. Disgusting comments, you know? Like that's all that matters about us." I took a deep breath. "And I think Tori's brother started it."

"Whoa," he said. "I don't even know what to say. And you haven't shown anyone?"

I shook my head. "I'm too afraid. But I want to do something. I just don't know what." I looked at him. "Any ideas?"

"How many girls?"

"I don't know," I told him. "I didn't count. Maybe a hundred?"

"What if you made copies and passed it out to all of them?" he suggested. "You'd have an army of girls ready to help you."

"An army of girls?" I repeated. That could be—"

I was going to say *interesting*. But Dion finished the sentence for me.

"Powerful. Hazel, think about it. A hundred girls coming forward and saying things about how our school needs to change? Some boys at our school think they can do anything or say anything and get away with it, right? You could show them that they're wrong."

I pulled out a piece of paper.

One honey bee is
nothing much, but a million?
Good pollinators!

Dion grinned big and wide after he read my latest haiku. "Exactly!"

"Okay, so I need to tell them," I said. "Tell some other girls. But how? I don't want to do it at school. I want to do it somewhere away from here. Where we can talk about it and decide what to do next without worrying some boy is gonna come around the corner any second."

While I'd been talking, Dion had devoured most of his sandwich. I hadn't eaten a thing. I knew I needed to, but thinking about all this made my stomach feel like I'd just gotten off the Zipper ride at the carnival. I picked up an apple slice and nibbled on it.

"Maybe you should have a party," he suggested.

"A party? But we're not celebrating anything. I mean, it won't really be a fun thing, will it?"

"A girl power party," he said. "Could be *kinda* fun, don't ya think?"

"A girl power party," I repeated, trying out the words for myself. I liked the sound of that.

"Dion?"

"Yeah?"

"You're brilliant."

He laughed. "Nah. I just like helping."

If only our school could be filled with people like Dion.

CHAPTER TWENTY-SIX

When Dad and I walked into the house after school, it smelled really good. Like freshly baked cookies. And that's because there was a plate of warm chocolate chip cookies and a glass of milk on the kitchen table. Mom was sitting there with a book.

"Are these for me?" I asked as I took a seat.

She smiled, causing the little lines by her big brown eyes to crinkle. "I figured you could use a little treat after your tough morning. I'm proud of you, Hazel. I know letting Pip go wasn't easy."

Dad grabbed a cookie and said, "I have a bit more work to finish up. See you in an hour or so, okay?"

"Okay," Mom and I said.

After he left, Mom asked, "Honey, are you all right?"

"Is it all right if we don't talk about it?" I asked. "Tori and I already talked about it after school, and I started crying again."

"Again? Does that mean you cried after you left him with Ms. Lennon?"

I nodded.

"Oh, sweetie, I'm so sorry. Okay, you need to think about other things. So besides that, how was school today? Anything fun or exciting happen?"

I wanted to say, "That would be a true miracle," but I didn't.

I'd been thinking about what might happen if I told my mom about the notebook. I worried that if she knew about it, she'd want me to do something that would be hard for me. She didn't seem to care about being embarrassed, but I did. Sure, the girls and I would probably have to do something hard, like talk to the principal. We could make a plan and do it together, though. But the thought of my mom and me walking into that office? It was more than enough to keep me from telling her.

"Not really. Though I did want to ask you if it'd be all right if I have some girls over on Friday? It's a teacher work day, remember, so there isn't any school."

I broke a cookie in half. I loved seeing the melted chocolate stretch and then break. I took a bite, and whoever said chocolate makes everything better was exactly right.

"Absolutely," she replied. "I asked for the day off months ago, so I'll be around. What's going on? Do you have a school project or a test to study for?"

I shook my head. "I just . . . I want to get to know some of the girls better. That's all."

"Great! I can help you make some snacks if you'd like."

"Okay. I'm not really sure what I want to do yet, but I'll let you know."

"Tori might want to help," she said.

"Well, probably not, because I'm not going to invite Tori. I kind of want to get to know some other people without her here."

Mom looked surprised, but she didn't argue with me. "All right. Just let me know if there's anything I can do."

I finished my cookies and milk and then got up to take my dishes to the sink. "I'm going to make the invitations right now. Can I use the computer?"

"Sure." She stood up. "Oh, wait, I might have a document I need to close out. I was taking notes earlier while I was on the phone."

"About your case?" I asked.

"Yes. About the case."

One of the things I'd been thinking about a lot was how the boys at school might treat me if they found out I was the one who'd found the notebook and got the girls together. It scared me. Hopefully we'd have a big group and there wouldn't be just one girl targeted. But with my mom . . .

"Is it hard to go to work with that going on?" I asked.

She sighed. "I'm not going to lie, it has been difficult. But I know I'm doing the right thing, so I remind myself of that all the time. And I love my job and talking to our customers, so I try to stay focused on that. But there have been a couple of awkward moments.

"Here's the thing, Hazel. Life is rarely easy. So we just have to do the best we can to get through the difficult moments and be thankful that we don't have hundreds of them every single day, like so many other people. You know we are pretty fortunate, right?"

My parents have always told me that we are blessed to have a roof over our heads, good food to eat, and a nice community with excellent schools. Still, it's easy to forget that some kids have it a whole lot worse than I do.

"I know. You're right."

She walked over and kissed the top of my head. "I love you, sweetie. Forever and ever. Times a million."

"Love you, too."

"Now, let me close that document out so you can make your invitations."

She went to the desktop computer that sat on a small desk on the edge of our kitchen. When she was done, she said, "All yours!"

I sat there for a long time, trying to figure out what to say. Finally, I added a graphic I found on the Internet with the words *Girl Power* with a pink background and three cartoon fists raised in the air. I put that at the top of the page and then below it typed in the date and time along with my name and address. Below all the details I wrote, "It's a Girl Power Party! Come for snacks and to talk about how we can make our school a better place for girls."

I played around with font colors and sizes until I was

happy with it. Then I saved it and printed out fifty copies. A hundred seemed like too many, because what if eighty of them came? We didn't have room in our little house for eighty people. It'd be tight if even thirty girls decided to come.

I planned on spending the evening folding the papers and taping them up. I'd decided it would be easiest to invite girls who were in my classes. That way, I didn't have to figure out who certain girls were, since I didn't know many names of the seventh and eighth graders. Some of them would be in the notebook and some of them wouldn't be, but hopefully it wouldn't matter that much. What mattered was that we figured out a way to make our school a better place for all of us.

It was really too bad that the invitations hadn't been ready that morning so I could have done most of the work with Tori absent. Except I hadn't even known I was going to have the party then. Dion had helped me so much—what a good friend.

With the invitations done, I went to my room. My eyes immediately went to the spot where Pip's box used to be. The room felt so empty now. Lonely. I thought of Pip at the school. Would he mind being alone at night? Did they give him enough vegetables to last until morning? Did he miss me as much as I missed him?

I plopped down on my bed with a big sigh. He was fine. Fine! The kids had been so excited to have him in their class. He'd get way more attention than I could have given him.

Even so, that didn't mean I wasn't supposed to miss him. Sometimes we know things are for the best but have feelings about it all, anyway. Like, maybe you know it's for the best that you don't have cable like most everyone else in the world because that means you spend more time outside, and you love being outside. But when everyone's talking about some amazing award show or the best Hallmark Christmas movie ever, you still wish you had cable. For a little while, anyway. That's just how it is. It's normal. Right?

"I miss you, Pip," I whispered. "And I'm sorry."

Why did everything lately have to feel so . . . wrong?

CHAPTER TWENTY-SEVEN

After I crawled into bed, I turned to my friend Pippi
Longstocking for some comfort. I'd always wondered what
it must be like to be Pippi. She's not afraid to say what's on
her mind. Not only that, but she makes it seem so easy,
though it's probably not easy at all. Like, when she walked
into a shop that had a sign that read DO YOU SUFFER FROM
FRECKLES? advertising a cream that could supposedly help
get rid of them, she spoke her mind. Pippi wanted to make
sure the shopkeeper knew that there's nothing wrong with
freckles, since she had them all over her face.

"I don't suffer from them. I love them," she told the
shopkeeper, followed by an enthusiastic "Good morning!"
Somehow, she did it nicely but still made her point. How
did she do that? And how come I couldn't be like that?

I hadn't forgotten what Dion had said. "When I'm
dancing, I tell myself I'm not Dion. I pretend I'm someone
else."

Although I'd managed two words with Preston and
Aaron, I was probably going to need more than that in the
coming days. So maybe I needed to pretend to be Pippi

Longstocking: strong, smart, and fearless. That's what I wanted to be.

What would Pippi have done if she'd found the note-book? She probably would have marched right out to that table where Tori's family had been eating spinach pizza, slapped it on the table, and said to Ben, "This is not okay, and I would like to know what you're going to do about it to make it right. Good evening!"

I thought of Pippi the next day at school as I used my ninja skills to hand out the invitations. I passed them around to girls in most of my morning classes, except first period, because Tori was in that class with me. Most of the girls looked very confused at first, like I was handing them a recipe for mud pies. But once they'd read them, I got a lot of smiles and thumbs-up.

At lunch, Dion arrived before Tori. I talked quickly. "Before she gets here, I want you to know that I'm doing it. I'm having a girl power party at my house Friday morning."

He held up his hand for a high five. "You go, girl. Proud of you."

I opened my lunch and gave him a bag of M&M'S that I'd picked up for him at the Plaid Pantry, our corner conve-nience store. "Couldn't have done it without you."

He looked at the candy and then back at me. "You got that for me?"

"Yes! Why wouldn't I? I'm pretending to be Pippi Longstocking, thanks to you."

"Pippi who?"

Just then, Tori walked through the doors. "Never mind," I whispered. "Just act normal."

As Tori sat down, Dion pulled a crumpled piece of paper from his pocket. "Hazel, I tried writing a haiku last night. You make it look so easy, but this thing took me at least an hour."

"Can I read it?" I asked. "Please?"

"Yeah, me too!" Tori said.

"Okay, sure," he said. "I know you'll be nice even if it's bad. And then I want to stick it in a book like Hazel usually does. Y'all know how thrilling that seems? Someone's gonna open a book and find a haiku that I wrote? Like, seriously?"

"I think we've got ourselves another haiku ninja," Tori said. "I'm feeling a little left out."

Dion grabbed a pencil along with a piece of scrap paper the librarian left out for us. He pushed both toward Tori. "There you go. Always room for more haiku ninjas in the world."

"I don't know," Tori said. "I'm not a very good writer. Math is more my thing."

"Have to try it and see," he said. "You never know. It felt funny to me at first, but then I really got into it. And instead of my brain having a pity party, I put it to work coming up with a little poem and it's like that's just what it needed." He ripped open the bag of M&M'S I'd given him. "Just like right now we need some chocolate to help us get through the rest of the day."

He poured some into each of our palms. As I popped the candies into my mouth, I read what he'd written:

> When birds get angry,
> they can fly to distant lands.
> I have bird envy.

"Wow, Dion," I said. "That's really good."

"Nah," he replied. "You're just saying that."

"No, she isn't," Tori said. "I can't believe that's your first one."

Dion shrugged as he threw an M&M into his mouth. "Took me a long time, though."

"As long as it's good, what does it matter?" I asked.

"But, Dion, what are you angry about?" Tori said.

My stomach felt funny all of a sudden. She shouldn't have asked that. If Dion had wanted to tell us, he would have told us. It wasn't right to ask him to explain why he'd written the haiku in the first place. It could have been really personal. Maybe even too personal to share. Should I say something? Would Pippi say something?

My brain whispered, *You spoke up to those two awful boys, which means you can speak up right here with your best friend.*

I swallowed hard before I said, "You don't have to tell us

if you don't want to. It's okay. We'll understand. Right, Tori?"

Tori replied, "Well, sure, but maybe he wants to tell us about it."

"I get mad that people call me names," Dion said. "That people can't see past the color of my skin. That some people at this school pick on others all the time and don't ever get caught." He paused. "That's about most of it, I guess."

"That's more than enough," I said.

"No kidding," Tori said.

Just then, a girl walked into the library and looked around. I recognized her from my social studies class. When she spotted me, she came over to where we were sitting.

She waved the paper around and said, "Hazel, I just wanted to say, I'm really glad you're doing this. I'm going to be there, and I'll bring a couple of friends, okay?"

Tori gave me a funny look. "Going to be where?"

Right then, I wanted to be a tortoise more than a human or an elephant or anything. Because all I wanted to do was tuck myself inside a shell and stay there for a very, very long time.

CHAPTER TWENTY-EIGHT

I looked at the girl and back at Tori and at the girl again. I tried my best to smile. "Glad you can come! Thanks for letting me know."

"No problem," she said. "See you Friday."

After she left, Tori said, "Hazel, are you going to tell me what's going on or not?"

I cleared my throat nervously. "I, um, want to get to know some other people at school better. That's all."

The look on her face told me she wasn't buying it. "But why didn't you invite me?"

"Because . . . I forgot?"

She shook her head. "I don't believe you. You didn't want me to come for some reason. What, are you embarrassed? Embarrassed to be seen with your friend who loves to do stupid karaoke? Or maybe you want the popular girls all to yourself."

"Tori, are you kidding? Does that sound like me?"

She stood up and picked up her hot lunch tray. "Something's going on with you. I don't know what it is, but I thought we told each other everything." Her bottom lip started to quiver. When she spoke, her voice was soft and shaky. "I've tried so hard to help you lately, Hazel. I thought we were best friends."

"Tori, we are! I'm sorry, I—"

But she didn't stay to hear what I might have to say. Which was for the best because I probably would have just messed things up even more.

I put my head in my hands while Dion said, "Uh-oh," like he was the one who'd just gotten caught in a big, fat lie.

"It's okay, Hazel," he said after we were quiet for a long time. "She's just upset right now. She won't stay that way forever."

I raised my head and looked at him. "I'm a horrible person."

"No. No, you're not."

"Why did I think I'd be able to keep it a secret? What was I thinking?"

"Anything I can do?" Dion asked.

"Unless you have magical powers that will rewind time, I don't think so."

"It's gonna be okay. Just give her some time. And then . . ."

"And then what?"

"Uh . . ." He squinted his eyes like he was thinking hard. But I think he was probably just afraid to say it. Afraid it'd freak me out because it was the exact thing I'd been trying to avoid.

"It's fine," I said. "You don't have to tell me. I already know."

"You do?"

"Yeah. I need to give her some time, and then I'm gonna have to tell her the truth. About the notebook."

He picked up a pencil and a piece of paper and started writing. I tried to eat more of my lunch, but I wasn't hungry anymore. When he'd finished, he pushed the paper over for me to read.

> A good friend likes you
> even when you make mistakes.
> We all make mistakes.

It was a very sweet thing to do. Like, just reading that made me feel a tiny bit better. "Thanks," I told him. "I hope it's true."

"It is," Dion said. "I really think it is."

"So, how much time, exactly?"

"I dunno. Couple of days, maybe?"

I sighed. "I want to text her right now."

"Here, let me give you my number. Text me instead."

We exchanged numbers and then it was time to go. "Dion?"

"Yeah?"

"Thanks for being a good person."

He smiled. "Takes one to know one."

When we walked out into the hall, I spotted Tori talking to some friends from our soccer team. She glanced at me but turned back really fast, like even making eye contact with me made her sick.

If so, we had that in common, because I definitely felt sick.

CHAPTER TWENTY-NINE

Tori has always been the person I could count on. No matter what.

There was the time I invited her to the beach with my parents and me. Tori and I both had kites, but mine broke. "Here, take mine," she'd said. "I like watching it fly just as much as flying it."

Or the time in fourth grade when our teacher told us that participating in the science fair wasn't optional but required, and I couldn't think of anything that hadn't been done already. Tori came up with an awesome idea, though: to try a bunch of different kinds of bubble gums and see which one made the biggest bubble. We had to work together, so one person could blow the bubble and the other person could measure it.

I couldn't help but think how incredible it was that she'd turned something I didn't want to do into something so fun, I didn't want the experiment to end.

Then there was the time I missed a whole week of school because I had the flu. Not only did she bring me my homework, but she also brought me a big container of chicken noodle soup that she'd helped make. It was the best chicken soup I've ever had.

In elementary school, I'd watched quite a few friendships end between girls, and I'd always wondered what had happened that was so bad—while at the same time feeling super thankful that I'd always have Tori. I was so sure nothing would ever happen to us.

And yet, here we were. And it was all my fault.

When I got home from school, Mom and Dad were both at work. Mom usually gets the early shift so she's home in the afternoons, but once in a while they ask her to work later.

I found a note on the counter.

Hi Hazel,
Please unload the dishwasher after you have a snack. I'll be home in time for dinner. Call Dad if you need anything!
Love you,
Mom

As I put the dishes away, my heart missed Pip and Tori so much I wanted to cry, and I thought about how to tell Tori the truth about everything. Today was Tuesday. Tomorrow and Thursday, we'd have soccer practice after school. And Friday was the party. It seemed like I was going to have to talk to her at school, which was going to be horrible. Where could we go so that people wouldn't overhear us? And even if I did find a place, would Tori even agree to listen to what I had to say?

Maybe I couldn't wait after all, like Dion had suggested. Maybe I needed to do it now. Like, right now.

If I surprised her and showed up at her house, she couldn't just slam the door in my face. Could she? No, she wouldn't do that. I knew Tori better than almost anyone, and even if I hadn't seen her angry that often, I knew she would at least hear me out. For a little while, anyway.

One of Tori's favorite things in the whole world is Swedish Fish. So before I headed to the garage to get my bike, I grabbed some money from the drawer where Mom keeps emergency takeout cash.

I rode a few blocks to the Plaid Pantry and parked my bike. I couldn't believe my luck. My very bad luck. Just as I was walking in, Aaron and Preston walked out.

Preston glared at me as he said, "Are you following us, Hazel? Do you like us so much that you miss us when we're gone?"

"No," I said firmly. "Leave me alone."

I walked through the doors and into the store. Once inside, I went to the candy aisle and smiled. Last time, I'd managed to get out two words. This time, four words!

It felt like I was sticking my neck out a little more each time. Moving forward, like Mom had said. I just hoped I could keep going.

I paid for the Swedish Fish and then hopped on my bike and rode to Tori's house.

But what I hadn't thought about, what I hadn't prepared for, was what to do if Ben answered the door. And that's exactly what happened.

"Hi," I said. "Can I talk to Tori, please?"

He stepped onto the porch and shut the door behind him.

"Where is it?" he hissed. "I want it back. Right now."

"Ben, I . . . I don't know what you're talking about."

"You're lying. You took it. You had no right to do that. It belongs to me. Do you know I could go to the police and file a report? I could charge you with theft."

Just then, the door opened and Tori appeared.

"Ben?" Tori said. "What's going on?"

He stepped aside to make room for all three of us. "Well, Hazel borrowed my protractor at school and I, uh, need it back. So I was just telling her to bring it to me tomorrow." He turned to me. "Like, you can't forget. You understand? It's important."

I nodded.

"Good," he said with a smug smile. "I'm glad we got that straight. See you girls later."

He went back inside and left the two of us standing there.

"What are you doing here?" she asked.

I handed her the Swedish Fish. "There may be plenty of fish in the sea, but I only have one best friend. And I'm sorry. I'm sorry I didn't tell you about the party. I have a good reason, though, and I want to tell you about it. If you'll let me."

She crossed her arms over her chest. "Okay. I'm listening."

I reached behind her and shut the door so we were alone on the porch. The last thing I needed was for Ben to overhear our conversation.

"I found a notebook. It's filled with girls' names from our school along with ratings and comments about their looks. Know what they said about me? 'Literally the worst' and 'uuuugly.' It's pages and pages of stuff like that. Well, unless you're gorgeous, then they carry on like the only reason girls are put on this earth is for boys to drool over you."

"That's . . . disgusting," she said. "Am I in there?"

I shook my head. "No. But lots of other girls are. And that's why I'm having girls over to my house on Friday. We need to figure out what to do about it. Not just that, but about the jerk problem at school and the stupid dress code. It's all connected, you know? Things have to change, and I want to do something."

"So do I," Tori said. "You should know that. Even if I'm not in the notebook, why wouldn't you invite me? And why didn't you show me the notebook when you found it? Why'd you keep it to yourself?"

I grabbed on to the railing that went around her front porch. This was going to be the hard part. The part I didn't want to do. I didn't want to tell her the rest. But I had to. There was no way out.

"Because I found it here," I said, trying to keep my voice calm. "At your house."

She gave me a funny look. "Here? I don't understand. That doesn't make sense."

"Ben had it," I explained. "But now I have it."

She stared at me for a moment before she said, "No. I don't believe you. Ben wouldn't do that."

"It's true, Tori. I swear."

I thought she might cry. Or yell for Ben and demand an explanation. Or pound the door with her fists out of anger. But she didn't do any of that.

Instead, she turned around, went back inside her house, and left me standing there. Alone.

CHAPTER THIRTY

When I got home, I texted Dion.

Me: **I told her. About the notebook and her brother. She's really mad.**

Him: **Uh oh. Probably should have let her cool off.**

Me: **I thought now would be better.**

Him: **Maybe she'll ask Ben about it.**

Me: **What if he lies?**

Him: **You show it to her. You got proof.**

Me: **I feel like I've lost her forever.**

Him: **It'll be ok. Maybe you should write her a haiku. Win her over with your beautiful** words. Or something.

Me: **Why did I even have to find that notebook? I'm not the right person for this.**

Him: **Bet you every single person who has done something big in their lives to help other people thought the exact same thing. You can do it, Hazel. Who you gonna pretend to be?**

Me: **Pippi Longstocking, like I told you.**

Him: **It sounds like a brand of socks. A bizarre brand of socks.**

Me: **Nope. She's a character from a book. So just call me Pippi from now on.**

Him: **Um, do I have to?**

Me: **No. JK. See you tomorrow.**

Him: **Ok.**

When Mom got home a little while later, I was sitting at

the table eating a slice of banana bread with peanut butter spread on it.

"You okay, honey?" she asked as she hung her purse on the back of one of the chairs. "You look like you've lost something very dear."

"I think that's exactly what's happened," I told her.

She sat down across from me. "What is it? What's going on?"

The thing was, I'd done everything I could think of to help myself and the other girls at school. But with Ben's threats and Tori not speaking to me, it felt like my attempts to stay afloat weren't working. Like I'd been clinging to a raft for hours or even days and my arms couldn't hold on much longer. It seemed like it was time to get help or drown.

And so, I told her. I told her everything. I told her about finding the notebook, then trying to get it from Ben at school and failing, and eventually, stealing it from Ben's bedroom. And how he'd threatened to go to the police if I don't give it back to him. I told her the real reason for the party on Friday and why I hadn't invited Tori and that she'd found out and was really angry with me.

After I finished, Mom sat there with her hands folded on the table, looking at her fingernails like they were going to start talking to her any moment. Finally, she said, "That notebook is a horrible thing. And I'm sorry you stumbled upon it. But stealing is wrong, sweetheart."

I nodded. "I know. So do you think I should . . . ?" It hurt to even say it. "Do you think I should give the notebook back?"

"I think what we need to do is talk to Ben and his moms. We need to just put everything out on the table, so to speak. They need to know so they can figure out what to do about it."

"He's going to be so mad at me," I whispered.

"But he's already mad, right? Besides, that's not a good reason to not act. Sometimes we have to—"

I knew what she was going to say. "Stick our necks out?"

She smiled. "Exactly. In the long run, this will help Ben. It really will."

"What about my girl power party?" I asked.

"You can still have it. I think it'll be good for you girls to get together and talk about things. It's pretty worrisome that you have some boys at your school who don't think there's anything wrong with talking about girls like that." She paused. "You were right to be alarmed. That kind of culture is called toxic masculinity, and it can lead to even worse behavior down the road."

"Behavior that makes you feel like you have to tell me to stay safe and be alert all the time?"

She frowned as she nodded. "Exactly."

"So, will you call Alice and Jeanie and set up a time for us to talk, or do I have to do it? Because I'm not sure what to say, really."

"I can do it," She pulled out her phone from the back pocket of her black work pants. "In fact, there's no time like the present."

CHAPTER THIRTY-ONE

Thursday night, after soccer practice, Mom, Jeanie, Alice, Ben, and I sat at their dining room table. Jeanie and Alice had asked that Tori stay in her room while we talked. Maybe they'd thought it would be even harder for me to share what had happened with her sitting there. Or maybe they'd wanted to keep it to as few people as possible for Ben's sake. The more eyes on him, the harder it'd be, probably. Whatever the reason, I was sort of glad for it. One less thing for me to worry about. I hoped with my whole heart that Tori and I would make up soon, but in the meantime, I was on a mission—a mission to fix what was wrong at our school. I had no idea if the girls and I could figure out what to do on Friday, but we were going to try, and maybe that's all that mattered.

I took a sip of the ice water Alice had gotten for all of us. There was also a plate of snickerdoodles in the middle of the table for us to share, but I was too nervous to eat. I'd hardly eaten anything all day. All I wanted was for this to be over.

"Thank you for meeting with us," Mom said. "I just

thought the best thing to do was to sit down and talk about what's happened and figure out where we go from here."

"Of course," Jeanie said. "Though we're completely in the dark, just so you know. If Ben knows what this is about, he hasn't said anything to us."

As nervous as I was, it probably wasn't even close to how Ben felt. He looked as white as a ghost.

"Hazel, can you tell them what you found, please?" Mom asked.

I'd stuffed it into the bag I took to soccer practice right before we'd left the house. Then I'd brought the bag inside with me. I reached down and pulled it out and set it on the table. As soon as Jeanie and Alice read the words on the front cover, they looked worried. Very worried.

"I found this notebook where boys at school rate girls on their looks and write stuff about them."

"May I?" Alice asked.

I nodded.

She reached over and pulled the notebook toward her. She opened it and read the inside cover. "Oh no," she whispered.

"Where did you find it, exactly?" Jeanie asked.

"In your bathroom," I said softly. "And then I came back and took it from Ben's room. I'm very sorry, but I . . ." How could I explain it? How could I make them understand? "I didn't want it passed around school anymore. It was the only way I could think of to stop it."

"You had no right to do that," Ben said. I swear his face had gone from white to cherry red in a matter of seconds.

Jeanie turned to Ben, tears welling up in her eyes. "Why would you think this is okay? I don't understand. How could you possibly think there's nothing wrong with doing something like this?"

Ben pursed his lips together for a moment, like he wasn't sure if he should say what he was thinking. But then, I guess he decided he better say something.

"There are a few guys who keep saying things about the two of you. Said I'd never be a man because I have two moms and no dad. I thought this would show them. I thought this would show them that I'm like everyone else."

It didn't make sense to me. "But you have so many friends," I blurted. "Why do you care what a few jerks say?"

As he stared at the plate of cookies, I wondered if he was trying to find the right words to explain it all. But when he finally replied, all he said was "I guess I don't really know."

Alice shook her head. She looked so angry, her eyes narrow as she glared at her son. "Benjamin Isaiah Robinson, are you saying you thought degrading girls and reducing them to a number was the only way you could think of to combat a few bullies? Because if that's true, I'd say we need to work on your problem-solving skills some more. Like, a lot more."

"Look, it was just a fun thing for us guys to do," Ben said. "I never thought a girl would see what we wrote. We weren't trying to hurt anyone's feelings. Don't you get it? That's why it says 'Private Property' on the front."

Meanwhile, Jeanie wasn't trying to stop the tears anymore. They streamed down her face. "There's no excuse for this. None. I thought we raised you to know better. To do better. My gosh, Ben, this is not how you treat girls. Ever. EV-ER!"

"You know what this is like?" Alice asked as she looked at Ben. "This is like you slapping us in the face. That's how it feels, reading this. Like everything we believe, everything we stand for as women, means nothing to you. You see how hard we fight every day for people to treat us as equals. I know you do. And you go and do something like this?"

Ben stared at the table. "I'm sorry," he finally said. "I didn't think about it, I guess."

"That's for sure." Jeanie turned to me. "I'm sorry you had to read all that, Hazel. I'm sure it must have hurt. Are you all right?"

"I think so," I said. "And I'm sorry for taking it. I should have told you about it instead of doing that. I just . . . I was scared."

"We accept your apology," Jeanie said.

"Yes," Alice said. "We forgive you. It's okay."

Mom stood up. "Hazel, I think we should go. They need some time to work through this as a family."

Alice pointed at the notebook. "I think we'll keep this if that's okay with you. We should probably let the other parents know what their sons have been up to."

Ben's mouth dropped open. "What?"

"This is a big deal, Ben," Jeanie said. "There have to be consequences for everyone involved."

I felt such relief in that moment. The boys weren't going to get away with it. Hopefully most of the boys would be punished. But there was one thing I needed to do to feel even better about all this. "Would it be okay if we tore out the page about me?"

Alice opened the notebook, flipped the pages until she found my name, and shook her head as she read the words there. Then she ripped it out. "Do you want to keep it or should I throw it away?"

I reached out my hand. "I'll take it."

With that done, Mom said, "Okay, time to go."

I pointed down the hallway. "Hold on, I need to give Tori something."

I took a piece of paper out of my bag and hurried toward her room. Tori's door was shut. I thought about knocking and handing it to her, but I'd had enough drama for one night. So I slipped it under the door and hoped Jeanie and Alice wouldn't be the only ones to forgive me.

Best friends forever,
that's what they said about us.
I'm lost without you.

CHAPTER THIRTY-TWO

I thought Tori might text me that night, but she didn't. Mom and I stopped at the store on the way home and got juice and muffins for the party.

While she brought the groceries inside, Mom asked me if I'd run and get the mail from the box at the end of our cul-de-sac. It was dark, but the streetlights gave off enough light that I wasn't scared. Dad was in his office, since he had a conference call. He works in cyber security, and sometimes he has to talk to coworkers in India, which means early morning and late evening calls because of the time difference.

I grabbed the key from the key holder, ran down the street, and opened our mailbox. There were a few bills and a large manila envelope with my name on it.

For a minute, I was really worried. What if it had something to do with the notebook? What if some of the boys at school had learned I had it? But when I got back inside the house, I could read the words on the small return address label. It had come from Hoover Elementary School.

"What is that?" Mom asked as she put the bottles of juice in the fridge.

"I don't know," I said as I ripped the envelope open. "But it's for me."

I reached my hand inside and felt lots of papers. And when I pulled them out, I saw that Ms. Lennon's students had made me cards. Thank-you cards, many of them with a turtle colored on the front.

I opened one of the cards and read it. "I love Pip so much. He is so sweet. Thank you for giving him to us."

Another one said, "I've never known a tortoise before. But now I do and I have a new favorite animal. Thanks for trusting us with him."

Someone else had written, "I've never had a pet before even though I've always wished for one. Thank you for making my wish come true."

Mom stood back, watching me. When I looked at her, I had tears in my eyes. She came over and wrapped her arms around me. "There's so much good in the world, Hazel. Never forget that."

"I know," I said.

When Mom let go of me, she thumbed through the pile. She pulled something out from the bottom. "Did you see this?"

She handed me a typed letter with a photo of Pip at the bottom.

Dear Hazel,

I hope this letter finds you well. I wanted to personally tell you how much we're enjoying having Pip in our classroom. Along with line leaders, lunch helpers, and door holders, we will now be rotating the jobs of feeding Pip, cleaning his house, and letting him sit nearby during silent reading time every afternoon.

Yesterday a student asked me, "Did you know tortoises have been around since the age of the dinosaurs? Isn't that awesome?"

I told him it certainly is and then he said, "They were probably afraid of getting stepped on by the dinosaurs. But they made it, didn't they, Ms. Lennon?"

You see, this is a boy who has been picked on a lot. A kind, sweet boy who talks with a lisp, dislikes PE, and loves music class. But Pip has shown him that even the meek among us can survive, thrive, and be loved.

Thank you, Hazel. Thank you so very much. Please come and visit him any time; we'd love to have you!

Best wishes,
Ms. Lennon

I stared at the photo for a minute. Pip was in his house munching on a cucumber slice. He looked happy, which made me happy. But also sad because I missed him.

I put the cards and letter back in the envelope and headed toward my room.

"Hazel?"

I turned around. "Yeah?"

"Do you know what you're going to say when all the girls are here tomorrow?"

"Not yet. But I'm working on it."

She smiled. "Okay. Good luck. Whatever you say, remember I'm with you. A hundred percent."

"Thanks, Mom."

Maybe I didn't have a pet tortoise. And maybe my best friend would be mad at me for a while. But I had parents who loved and supported me, no matter what.

Was that another superpower grown-ups had? I wondered. Or maybe my parents were just pretty awesome. Yeah, that was probably it.

CHAPTER THIRTY-THREE

Our living room was packed. We'd set up folding chairs, but many of the girls stood along the walls and some sat on the floor. I was kind of shocked that so many had decided to come. I was just about to get started when the doorbell rang a few minutes after ten o'clock, the official start time.

I gasped when I opened the door and found Tori standing there, holding her karaoke machine.

"Hi," she said.

"Hi. I'm really glad you're here."

"I'm sorry," she said. "About everything."

"Same," I said. "It's been awful this week, trying to avoid you. I mean, not that I wanted to avoid you, I just thought you didn't want to be anywhere near me. So I pretended I had the measles and told myself it was important to stay away from you so you wouldn't get them, too."

She gave me a funny look. "You pretended you had the measles? Pretty sure you should have stayed in bed, then."

"It was a mild case. Like, super mild. I mean, look at me now! I'm perfectly fine!"

We both laughed.

"My brother told me to give you this." Tori reached into her pocket and pulled out a small crumpled envelope. "I think it's an apology. You can read it later, if you want."

"Okay." I stepped aside and held the door open as I took the karaoke machine from her and set it on the floor against the wall. "Come in. There's some juice and snacks at the table if you want anything." I pointed to the small table by the door. "Oh, and make yourself a name tag."

The girls had gotten a lot louder, which told me it was definitely time to get started.

I'd practiced in my room last night for a couple of hours. I knew what I wanted to say. It was just going to be hard saying it in front of so many people. If only I loved public speaking the way Tori loved singing. At least my teachers in elementary school had made us do short speeches every year. As much as I'd struggled at the time, they'd made me practice, and like Dad always says, "The more you practice, the better you get."

As I stood at the front of the room, I took a deep breath and reached into my pocket for my notes. "Thanks for coming, everyone," I said as loudly as I could manage, which wasn't very loud at all.

A bunch of girls said, "Shhhhhh," to help me, which was nice, and it wasn't long before everyone was quiet, their eyes on me.

I cleared my throat and then said, "I want to tell you the reason I've invited you here, and then we're going to break up into groups and hopefully have some fun." My voice was shaking, so I cleared my throat again and told myself to be like Pippi. Strong. Confident. Kind.

"Since it's a nice day," I continued, "we can go out back where there are blankets on the lawn." I glanced at Tori. "And when we're done with that, I think we'll do some karaoke, if that's okay."

Some girls applauded while others said "yes" and "fun!"

"I've found a couple of, um, interesting things the last few weeks," I said. "I found a lost turtle. He's now at Hoover Elementary in Ms. Lennon's class. The second thing I found was a notebook filled with names. Girls' names." I swallowed hard. "Your names. Some boys at our school were passing it around, rating us on our looks and making comments."

"What do you mean?" a girl named Lexi called out. "What do you mean, making comments?"

"I'll pass around the sheet with my name, so you can see what the notebook is like. The rest of it will be destroyed." I took the page with my name and passed it to the girl sitting nearby. "Some of the comments were nice and some were really terrible. But it doesn't matter. Like, girls shouldn't be happy if their comments were good, because it all means the same thing—they see us in one way and one way only. But we're so much more than how we look, you know?"

Most of the girls nodded.

"This is disgusting," one of the girls, Andi, said as she passed my page on to the next person.

I nodded. "The good news is that most of the parents of the boys involved are going to find out what's happened. And hopefully, there will be punishments. At first I thought that was the most important thing. But the more I've thought about it, the more I've realized it probably won't change anything at school. Like, yes, the boys were horrible to do this, except that we go to a school where this kind of thing seems normal.

"And see, for a while I had a tortoise named Pip. He taught me that in this world, we can either hide in our shells and go nowhere, or we can stick our necks out and help ourselves move forward. I decided, with everything I've seen since starting middle school—the dress code, the way girls are treated—that I couldn't hide in my shell, even if that would have been easier in some ways. Because our school is . . . um, well . . ."

Thankfully, my best friend could see I was struggling. Tori hopped up to stand next to me and said, "Our school has some problems. Big problems. And we need to do something about them."

At first, it was quiet. But then, someone started clapping, and others joined in until I swear the room was shaking from all the noise. I looked around at those faces, and my heart felt like it might burst.

When it quieted down again, Tori continued talking, which I was grateful for. "Every day, girls are getting sent home for what they wear. It's ridiculous. And Hazel and I are tripped by two boys in our hall who think it's a game. We've been called names by other boys. Hazel gets awful notes left on her music stand in class. I bet lots of you have stories like that, too."

Several heads nodded.

"Okay," I said, "so now that you know why you're here, let's go outside and get into groups. We need to come up with ideas on what to do to try and fix some of these problems."

"Are some of us going to have to talk to the principal?" Andi asked.

"Probably," I said.

Tori jumped in and said, "But maybe we shouldn't worry about that yet. Right now, let's just think of ideas on how to make our school better. Okay?"

It felt overwhelming. It felt like we were standing at the bottom of a big mountain and we had a long, hard climb ahead of us. But what Tori had basically said was, one thing at a time.

That's how we were gonna do this.

One thing at a time.

Together. All of us.

CHAPTER THIRTY-FOUR

While the girls went outside with their snacks, chatting as they went, Mom came over and put her arm around my shoulders and gave me a big squeeze. "I'm so proud of you, Hazel. Like, *so* proud! Did you hear yourself?"

I smiled. "Yeah. I did it, Mom. I really did it."

She kissed the top of my head. "You sure did. You found your voice, and I'm so glad you're using it."

"It's still scary," I whispered. "But one thing at a time, I guess."

"Exactly."

Most of the girls had broken up into groups and were sitting on blankets in the grass. I helped the few girls still standing find a group to join. Mom had also set out a small pad of paper and a pen on every blanket so the girls could write down any ideas they came up with.

"Don't worry about whether ideas or good or not," I told everyone. "Just write down anything you think of, big or small."

"Do you think we need a name?" someone called out. "Like, a name for our group?"

"No," I said. "Because this isn't just about us. It's about making the school better for everyone for a long, long time. I mean, hopefully that's what will happen."

I joined a group with four girls, and we went around and introduced ourselves. A couple of them I knew from Hoover, but the others I didn't know, although their names sounded familiar. Probably because I'd read their ratings.

"My name is Gina Tran. I'm a seventh grader, and I'm so glad to be here." She looked at me with her sad brown eyes. "Thank you, Hazel. We have to do something. We just have to."

The next girl was Maddie Gray, the gorgeous girl Tori had waved to at Ruby's when we were there last. I felt so bad for her. Just yesterday, I'd heard boys saying things about her. Gross things. Horrible things.

"Hi," she said. "I'm Maddie Gray. I'm in eighth grade. My younger sister, Hannah, is over there, in the purple shirt." She pointed to a blanket behind us. "My mom thought about pulling us out of public school and home-schooling us, but Hannah wanted to try it. From what she's seen since starting in September, she now understands why I've been complaining so much the last few years."

"I'm sorry," I told her. "I wish . . . I wish they weren't so mean to you."

She smiled. "It's not your fault. And hopefully, we're going to make things better."

I turned to the next girl. She said, "My name's Anastasia

and I'm in the sixth grade, like Hazel. I can't believe how horrible this school is, and I can't believe no one has done anything about it until now."

"And I'm Paris," the last girl said.

I pointed to her T-shirt, which read GIRLS CAN DO ANYTHING and told her, "I love that so much."

"Thanks," she replied. "I'm, uh, in the seventh grade and I am so here for this. I can't wait to get to work."

And that's what we did. We talked about how we wanted middle school to be: friendly, fun, nice, encouraging, fair. We talked about what we didn't want to see anymore: bullying, mean comments, name-calling, people thinking we're the problem because of how we're dressed, and lots more.

"It all seems so . . . big," Gina said after we'd made our lists. "The problems, I mean. And the way we want it to be is so far off from how it is."

"I know," I said. "But whatever we do will be better than doing nothing, right?"

"It's hard to not feel down about it all," Anastasia said.

"This is the most hopeful I've felt since I started middle school, though," Maddie said. "Like, we're gonna do something, you know? We're going to show those boys that it's not okay to treat us like dirt."

We managed to come up with a few ideas and after that, I stood up and asked all the groups to pass me their lists of ideas along with each girl's cell phone number and email address. "I want to make a list of all the ideas and have everyone vote on them. So I'll work on that this weekend and send it out, okay?"

"Hazel?" Paris said. "You should ask for volunteers to talk to the principal. You've done a lot. You don't have to do that, too."

"I'll volunteer," Maddie called out.

And then a chorus of "Me too"s followed.

So many girls who wanted to help me. Help us. Girls who wanted to do the right thing and give us a school where we didn't have to feel worried or afraid all the time. It made my heart so happy, I almost started crying.

"Thank you," I said. "But I want to talk to him, too. I found the notebook, so I should be the one to tell him about it, even if it'll be hard."

"We're with you!" Lexi called out.

Tori bounded over to where I stood. She looked at me, her hands pressed in front of her like she was begging. "Okay. So. With all that out of the way, is it time?"

"Yes!" I said.

She waved her hands in the air and yelled, "Yay, karaoke time!"

We spent the next hour singing and dancing and laughing. It was so much fun!

When it was all over, and Tori and I were the only ones left, I collapsed onto the sofa and said, "We did it. I can't believe it. But we did it."

Tori sat next to me and said, "No. That's not true."

"What?" I asked. "What do you mean?"

"*You* did it, Hazel. You got them here. You came up with what to say. You got them into groups. You got them talking. You got them to brainstorm ideas." She patted my leg. "It was all you, boo."

"I kind of feel like I suddenly have thirty-seven new friends," I said.

"You do," Tori said. "I know you do. And I bet it's just the beginning."

"I'm glad you came," I told her. "Really glad. And the karaoke machine was brilliant."

"Why, thank you," she said as she stood up and took a bow. "I agree, it was brilliant. I mean, you called it a party, so I figured we should do something fun besides figuring out how to smash the patriarchy."

"What's that mean?" I asked.

"Oh, it's something my moms say sometimes," Tori said. "Patriarchy is when men hold the power in society. And smashing it means—" She started laughing. "Well, you know what *that* means."

"I just want things to be equal," I said. "The same, you know? I want them to see us as people, not as girls who are cute or ugly."

She got serious all of a sudden. "I know my brother has apologized, but I just want to say, I'm sorry, too. I'm sorry he was involved in that."

"I know. He seemed pretty horrified that your moms were going to contact the other parents."

"Well, that's not all," Tori said. "They've also told him he has to read one book a month and write a report each time about what he's learned. Books about gentle and kind boys. Books about girls doing incredible things. Books that make him really think, you know?"

I smiled. "I like that. Maybe he should read *Pippi Longstocking*. She's kind of my hero."

"Hmm. Maybe I'll suggest that. So, we're still going to Dion's later, right? Want to meet up and ride together or . . ."

"Tori, I'm not sure—"

She waved her finger. "Oh no. No! You were just out there dancing like it was no big thing. And Dion needs you!" She waited for me to say something, but what was there to say? "Just come and try it with us. Please?"

"Okay."

"Awesome! Text me later, 'k?"

"Yeah. See you later."

After she left, I took out Ben's note and read it.

DEAR HAZEL,

WHAT WE DID WAS WRONG. I KNOW THAT NOW. EVEN
IF WE NEVER MEANT FOR ANY GIRL TO READ WHAT WE
WROTE, IT WAS WRONG AND I'M SORRY. CAN I BAKE
YOU SOME CUPCAKES TO TRY AND MAKE UP FOR IT? I'LL
BE AT YOUR SOCCER GAME SATURDAY. TEXT MY

SISTER AND LET HER KNOW WHAT FLAVOR YOU WANT
AND I'LL BRING SOME FOR YOUR TEAM.

SORRY,
BEN

Cupcakes? He was going to make *us* cupcakes? Now, that was more like it!

CHAPTER THIRTY-FIVE

"Come on in and make yourselves right at home," Dion's grandma told us when she opened the door. She was short and wore red lipstick to match her glasses, which looked good with her dark skin and short, curly hair. She had on a gray tracksuit and held a book in her hand.

A little black dog, a schnauzer I think, wagged its tail and came over to greet us when we stepped inside the old house. It smelled good, like cake baking in the oven.

"Hi!" Tori said, bending down to pet the dog.

"That's Jack," Dion's grandma told us.

"Hi, Jack," I said, stooping down to give him a pat, too.

Just then, a much taller woman with her black hair piled high in a bun came around the corner with Dion and another boy.

"Hi!" Dion said. "Grandma and Mama, this is Hazel and Tori. Hazel and Tori, this is my grandmother and my mother. And this here's my brother, Kalen. Pop's at work, so you can't meet him today."

"Please, call me Dorothy," his grandma said.

"And you can call me Stacy," his mom said.

While Tori went over to shake their hands, I said softly, "Nice to meet you."

Stacy smiled. "Dion tells me you've been kind and welcoming to him. I sure do appreciate that. I'm always telling him it's not what people think of you that matters. It's what you *do* and how you treat others. So thank you for being a good example to him."

"Well," Tori said, "he's a good egg, and we're glad to have him as our friend."

That made Dorothy's face light up. "He sure is, isn't he? Except he won't kill spiders for me. Just found a big one in my bedroom I had to get rid of myself. Gonna have to work on that." She winked at us to let us know it wasn't that big of a deal.

"Spiders *and* mice?" I teased.

Kalen looked at Dion. "You told them about the mouse?"

Dion shrugged. "They wanted to know why I hate mice, so I told them. Plus, it's a good story."

"Yeah, 'cause you weren't the one who got bit," Kalen said.

"What about snakes?" Tori asked Dion. "You hate snakes, too?"

"Forget snakes," I said. "How about elephants?"

"Love elephants!" Dion exclaimed.

I smiled. "Then you're good."

"Kalen, you need to let your brother and his friends practice," Stacy said. "So you finish cleaning your room, you hear me? I'm in the sewing room finishing up that baby blanket I'm making for the shower tomorrow. You kids just let me know if you need anything, all right?"

Dorothy said, "I've got to get ready for my shift at the hospital. Y'all can help yourselves to a brownie if you'd like. Should be cool enough by now."

Kalen ran to the kitchen and grabbed a brownie, then bolted upstairs. Dorothy and Stacy both went down the hall and around the corner.

"She made us brownies?" I asked.

"Yeah, she loves to bake," Dion said. "She's been teaching me recipes, too. Back in Alabama, our next-door neighbor taught me how to bake a peach pie so I'd make them in the summertime, but Grandma's teaching me a lot more. See, my mama isn't a very good cook. And my pop, well, he's good with the barbeque, but that's about it. Come on, let's grab a brownie and go upstairs."

We each took a brownie and a napkin and walked toward the gorgeous wooden staircase in the middle of the house. Even though the home was old, with its creaky wooden floors and a kitchen without a single modern-day appliance, the place was bright and welcoming. I felt right at home.

"This house is super cute," Tori told Dion. "I love it."

"Me too," Dion said. "My room's pretty small, but you can see it if you want. I thought we could practice in the attic. It gets hot in the summer, but it's fine today."

205

I nibbled on my brownie as we went while Tori and Dion had already finished theirs. It was soft and gooey and really delicious.

He opened a door, and we all stepped into his neat and tidy room. It had just a single bed with a brass headboard, a dresser, and a little white desk. On the dresser were a couple of soccer trophies. He'd also hung three posters on the walls.

"You must have been on some good teams," I said as I walked over to check out his trophies.

"I bet you have really good footwork, huh?" Tori said. "And that's why you're probably an amazing dancer."

He just laughed. "I mean, sure. I try, I guess."

"Who's that?" I asked, pointing at a white man in a tux and a white woman in a fancy dress dancing together.

"Fred Astaire and Ginger Rogers." He pointed to one of the other posters, this one with a black man wearing a suit and hat and kicking his heels up. "And that's Sammy Davis Jr."

"And now we know you're team cat." Tori said as she pointed to the last poster with six of the cutest kittens I'd ever seen, all piled together in a basket. "Maybe because they eat mice?"

"Got that right," he said. "'K, come on, let's go up to the attic."

We went up another flight of stairs into a room that had sloped ceilings and boxes and other stuff lined up along the walls. It was warmer than it'd been downstairs, and the air smelled kind of stale.

"So, how was the party?" Dion asked as he went over and opened a small window.

"It was good," I said. "At least I think it was."

"Yeah, really good," Tori said. "Think some of us are going to try and talk to the principal on Monday."

"Cool." Dion pointed to the bag Tori carried. "So, you bring a notebook of talent show tips or something?"

Tori reached in and pulled out an iPad. "I was thinking maybe we could watch some videos before we plan out what we're gonna do. I found some other people who've performed this song."

"Yeah, okay," Dion said.

There were some folded chairs up against one of the walls, so he grabbed them one by one and unfolded them for us so we could sit in a small circle.

Dion leaned back in his chair, his arms folded across his chest. "I'm curious, Tori. Why do you want to be in the talent show so bad, anyway?"

She shrugged. "I don't know. I just always thought it'd be fun. My brother's done it the past couple of years, and I don't want to be left out this year."

"You can say it," I told her.

"Say what?" she asked.

I picked at a hangnail on my pinky. "That you want to be popular. Even more popular than your brother."

She kind of stared at me for a minute before she said, "I . . . what?"

"It's true, right?" I swallowed hard. "I'm not enough anymore. You want more. It's okay. Just say it. I mean, he asked, right?"

Her mouth was still open and she kept staring. "That day you signed up," I said. "I saw how happy you were. Those girls hanging around the sign-up sheet, taking selfies, were more like you than me. And you want more of that. I know you do. I just want you to admit it. It's fine. I can eat lunch with Dion if you don't want to eat with us anymore."

"When did I say that?" she asked.

"I won't ever be popular, I can tell you that right now," Dion said, slumping down in his chair and stuffing his hands in the pockets of his hoodie. "I thought we were doing this talent show thing to make a statement or something."

"We are!" Tori said.

"Really?" I asked.

Now Tori's shoulders slumped. "Look, you don't know what it's like being his little sister."

"What do you mean?" Dion asked.

She bit her lip, like she was thinking hard about how to answer. Finally, she said, "I feel like everyone looks at me and judges me. Teachers. Coaches. Students. Everyone. I'm not as charming as him. Or as good-looking. Or as athletic.

And yes, not as popular as him. I just wanted . . ." She sighed. "Middle school felt like a new beginning. I wanted to try and prove that I'm just as good as him."

"But you don't judge people on how they look," Dion said. "Seems to me you're already good."

Dion amazed me. He said things in a way that made so much sense.

Tori stood up, put the iPad on her chair, and went and looked out the window at the end of the room. "I'm tired of being Ben Robinson's little sister. I want people to see me for *me*, you know? Especially now, after what's happened. Whatever he's done, good or bad, I'm trapped. Trapped as Ben Robinson's little sister."

I hadn't really thought of it like that and I felt a little guilty, to be honest. She was my best friend. How had I not known she felt that way? Since I didn't have any siblings, it was hard for me to know what it must be like, but I wanted to try.

"Like, if Abby Wambach were my sister," I said, "people would think of her when they saw me. They might even ask, 'Where's Abby?' and make me feel invisible."

Tori turned around. "Exactly. I guess I don't really care if we eat in the library the rest of the year. And I don't care if you're the only two friends I have, because you guys are awesome and I know I'm lucky. I'm just . . ."

Her voice trailed off.

"Tired of living in your brother's shadow?" Dion asked.

Tori bit her lip and looked like she was going to cry. "Yes."

Now Dion stood up. "Well, it's not gonna solve all your problems, but I guess our performance at the talent show is a good chance to step out on your own, so how about we get started?"

CHAPTER THIRTY-SIX

Saturday morning, as I walked toward the field, the sun peeking behind the clouds, Ben stepped onto the gravel walkway from the parking lot and walked alongside me. He had two pastry boxes in his hands.

"Where's Tori?" I asked.

"On the field already," he said. "I waited for you. Got your chocolate cupcakes with raspberry frosting. Just like you asked for."

"Thanks," I told him. "Can you keep them for me until after the game?"

"Sure," he said. "I really am sorry, Hazel. I'm sorry for being so rude to you, and for the notebook, too. I never meant for anyone else to see it. You get that, right? I never meant to hurt anyone's feelings. Especially yours."

"But it's horrible either way," I told him. "We're not just something pretty to look at or something ugly to laugh at, you know?"

"Yeah," he said. "I know. And you're probably gonna be mad for a while. Hopefully not forever, though."

That's when I had a thought. "If you want to help change

things at our school, you could come with us when we talk to the principal."

"Are you, um, gonna mention my name?"

I shook my head. "There are a lot of problems. The notebook is just one of them. All we want is for things to change. But I can't promise . . ."

"I get it. And I'll be there. Just let me know if there's anything specific I can do to help, okay?"

We'd reached the field. Tori waved at me and I waved back.

"Have a good game," he said.

And it *was* a good game. Close, but we won, two to one. And when the game was over, the girls loved the cupcakes. Ben still wasn't forgiven, but it was a start, I guess.

Afterward, we went home and Mom helped me set up a survey online so I could ask the girls who'd come to the girl power party to vote on their favorite ideas. By Sunday night, I had the results and couldn't wait to share them. I sent everyone an email with the top three ideas.

1. Training for all students about what toxic masculinity looks like and how to make changes at our school to keep it from happening
2. A poster contest where kids can make posters displaying positive messages with awesome prizes offered

3. A one book, one school program where everyone reads books highlighting girls

And then I wrote, *We need to decide on the team who will meet with the principal and vice principals. My mom said she'll call on Monday and arrange the meeting for us sometime this coming week. Who wants to go?*

I made a point to log on to my computer Monday morning before school and was surprised to find that twenty-seven girls had volunteered. I couldn't believe it. They knew it would be hard, but they were willing to do it, anyway. It was like I had a whole crew of Pippi Longstockings, and it made me feel like I could do anything. Anything!

As I walked into school, I felt good. Better than good. Amazing! Until it all came crashing down because Aaron and Preston greeted me just inside the doors.

"We've heard things about you, Hazel," Preston said.

Be Pippi, I told myself. "Whatever," I said. "I don't care."

"We've heard you're a snitch," Aaron said. "A blabbermouth. That you're gonna turn us all in."

"You know what happens to snitches?" Preston asked.

"I told you, I don't care!" I yelled as I rushed toward the sea of people in my hall, my heart racing. Thankfully, Tori was waiting at our locker and she could tell I was upset.

"Did something happen?"

"I'm so sick of them," I hissed. "I think Aaron and Preston are trying to scare me from saying anything to the principal."

"But how would they know?" she asked.

I shrugged. "Someone must have told them."

Tori pursed her lips. "Do you think Ben told them?"

"No," I said. "He seems to feel pretty bad about the whole thing. It could have been anyone. Like, some of the girls have brothers here, you know. If they went home after the party and talked about what we were doing, someone might have overheard and spread it around. Who knows?"

"Are you scared?" she asked.

"A little," I said. "But it won't stop me. I mean, we can't stop now, right? We have some good ideas and if we do nothing, then nothing changes."

"I really want things to change," Tori said. "So, so much."

"Yeah. Me too."

At lunch, we filled Dion in on the plan.

"Can I be in the group that talks to the principal?" he asked as he dipped his corn dog into some ketchup. "Like, maybe it'd be good for him to know it's not just girls getting bullied."

"Yes!" Tori said. "I like that. What do you think, Hazel?"

"Yeah, I like it, too. Thanks, Dion. I know it doesn't make it right, but Ben was kind of bullied, and that made him turn around and bully a bunch of girls. Like, it has all kinds of effects, you know?"

"It's so true," Tori said. "Okay, so the three of us will be at the principal's meeting. How are you going to choose the others?"

I tapped the small pieces of scrap paper sitting in the middle of the table. "I think I'm going to put the names on pieces of paper like this, put them in a hat, and draw them. I don't know what else to do. That seems the fairest. What do you think?"

"It might be good to make sure we have some from each grade. So if we are the sixth graders in the group, maybe just draw names for the seventh and eighth graders."

I nodded. "Yeah. Good idea." I put my baggy of carrot sticks on the table to share. "Mom is going to call today and make the appointment for us. Once I choose the names, we should meet up and talk about what we're going to say. Unless you want to write a song for us to sing, Tori."

Her eyes lit up. "Can I? Please? That'd be super fun!"

"Seriously?" I asked.

"Yes! Please? Pretty, pretty please?"

Dion and I answered at the exact same time. "No!"

"You big meanies," she told us. Then she winked. "Who I love with my whole heart."

I was so happy to have my best friend back.

CHAPTER THIRTY-SEVEN

With everything happening, I found myself missing Pip a lot. A whole, whole lot. So on my bike ride home, I decided to stop in at the school and see if Ms. Lennon was still there. I had texted Mom to let her know and she'd given her standard response. "Okay, stay safe. Be alert." I think it was just habit at this point.

I walked into the office and the secretary remembered me, which made me happy and sad at the same time. Hoover Elementary, and all the people in it, were the best, and it just wasn't fair I couldn't be a part of it anymore.

"Hi, Hazel," she said. "Stopping in to see Ms. Lennon?"

"Yes, is she still here, do you know?" I asked.

"I don't think I've seen her leave, so she's probably in her classroom. Go ahead and sign this visitor sheet and you can head down."

As I walked down the hallway, I stopped at the classroom where I'd seen my kindergarten buddy, River. The door was open, so I peeked inside to see if Mr. Knight was there. He wasn't. So I went in, dropped my backpack on the floor, and sat at one of the tables in one of the tiny chairs.

At every seat, there were drawings with captions about what they'd drawn. The one at the seat I was in said, "I hav a dog and a cat. I love tem. Esept wen the cat skrats me." She'd written her name at the top of the page in all capital letters— "CHLOE." And she'd drawn a picture of a dog and a cat.

I circled the picture with my finger, my heart aching for the days when school meant coloring pictures and reading picture books every day.

"You can draw one too, if you'd like."

I jumped out of the chair and turned around. Mr. Knight stood there in jeans and a green T-shirt that had a bright yellow bee and the word KIND right underneath it. Such a cute way to say, "Be kind."

"Oh no, that's okay," I said. "I came to visit Ms. Lennon. Sorry. I just . . ."

"You miss it a little?" he asked.

Tears filled my eyes. I wanted to say no. I wanted to say that everything was fine and I'd never felt better and I was excited about being in middle school where selfies ruled the world. But it wasn't true. Not even close.

"Yeah," I said softly. "But I shouldn't, right?"

As he walked toward his desk at the front of the room, he said, "I tell my own children all the time, everyone grows up differently. There's no right or wrong in how you do it. My seven-year-old still likes his mom to rock him a few minutes before bed. Not to sleep or anything. It's just their snuggle time, you know? Nothing wrong with it, though

217

I'm sure some adults would judge us if they knew. I figure, life is hard, and there are no rules about how we get through it. If a little cuddle time is what the kid needs, well, there are worse things in the world."

"I bet he'll grow up to be kind," I said. "Like your shirt says."

He smiled. "I sure hope so." He picked up some papers from his desk and then walked them over to me. "Here. You can do some at home later if you'd like."

They were three of the sheets with a blank space at the top for a picture and then lines below to write something about what you'd drawn.

I stuck them in my backpack. "Thanks," I told him.

"You're welcome."

When I walked into Ms. Lennon's room, I said hello and she looked up from her desk. "Oh, Hazel, what a lovely surprise."

"Thanks for the envelope of thank-you cards," I told her. "I really loved them. I'm so glad your students like Pip."

She stood up and smiled. "It's going so well. We really owe you a lot. I think everyone's behavior has already improved. Of course, I've made some other changes, too, but I know Pip is really helping. Oh, let me show you this writing project we've been working on."

We walked over to one of the students' desks where she showed me a piece of notebook paper with words written at the top: "What I've learned from Pip."

"They're writing so many incredible things," she told me. "Things like how to care for someone who can't take care of themselves. How to be gentle. How to love something that can't talk. But my favorite is probably from a boy who's had some problems at home, which was causing him to act out at school. One of the things he wrote was, 'Pip has taught me that it's okay to tell someone I'm scared or worried, like Pip shows people when he goes into his shell. People won't know unless I tell them.'"

"Wow," I said.

"I know, right?" she said.

"Pip taught me some things, too," I said. "Like, I'm sticking my neck out a lot more, thanks to him."

She looked genuinely happy. "Oh, Hazel, I love that. As hard as it is, we have to learn to do that to get what we need in this world."

I went over and picked up Pip and held him at arm's length. When his beautiful little eyes met mine, my heart melted. "I love you," I whispered as I pulled him close.

He couldn't say it back, but I knew he loved me, too. Sometimes words are important. But sometimes it's enough to just be there, without any words at all. I'm pretty sure Ms. Lennon knew that, because she let me hold him for a long time, the classroom as quiet as a field of daisies on a warm, sunny day.

CHAPTER THIRTY-EIGHT

When I got home, bad news was waiting for me. Before Mom even said anything, I knew by the look on her face that something was wrong.

"What is it?" I asked. "What's happened? Is Dad all right?"

"Oh, he's fine, he's in his office, working. It's just, I'm sorry to tell you this, but the principal wasn't very open to meeting with you and the other students. He said he'd rather meet with just you and me."

"But I don't want that," I said.

"I know, sweetheart. But I don't know what to do. He asked me what the meeting was about and I said that a large number of girls were upset about how boys were treating them. Then I told him I was calling to request a meeting with a small group of them, and he said he didn't think that would be an effective use of his time."

I stared at my mom with my mouth gaping open. "Say what?"

She sighed. "It's pretty unbelievable. I'm not sure what to do next, to be honest."

"He might as well have told us to email him our thoughts," I said. "He doesn't even care about us, does he?"

"I don't think that's entirely true," Mom said. "But we definitely have different views as to how much say parents and students should have in what happens at school."

I squeezed my fists that hung at my sides. "You know what? We'll just go there tomorrow and stand there until he'll see us. We are his students. He's supposed to be there to *help* us!"

"You sure you want to do that?"

"I'm positive. And you know what? I was wrong. A small group isn't the best way to do this. We need a big group. Like, the bigger, the better. Can I use the computer?"

Mom smiled. "It's all yours. Oh, and check the bag there. I bought you a gift and a few extras if you have any friends who would like one."

I pulled four T-shirts out of the bag. Two of them said MY BODY IS NONE OF YOUR BUSINESS. One said ALL YOU NEED IS LOVE, EQUAL RIGHTS, AND CUPCAKES. And the last one said I WILL NOT STAY QUIET.

It was going to be hard to choose just one. I loved them all!

I went to my room, emptied my backpack, and saw the sheets Mr. Knight had given me.

I shrugged. *Why not?* I said to myself.

Then I sat down at my desk and drew a picture of Pip. And underneath it I wrote, "Sticking your neck out is hard. But sometimes it really is the only way to move forward."

The next morning, a bunch of us met in the library. I'd chosen to wear the I WILL NOT STAY QUIET T-shirt, since that seemed to be the theme for the day. I was so scared to do this—to rally everyone and demand a meeting. But I knew doing nothing and watching nothing change would be a whole lot scarier.

I stood up and said, "Hi. Thanks for coming. So, at lunchtime, we'll all meet outside the library. And then we'll go to Mr. Buck's office together. Feel free to let any friends know about what we're doing. If they want to join us, they can. I feel like the more people we have, the harder it will be for him to say no. Like, he can't ignore a huge number of us, right?"

"Right!" Tori said because she's awesome like that.

I passed out copies of a list I'd made. "If we get the meeting, these are some of the ideas we're going to suggest. And I also think we should ask for a monthly meeting to talk about how things are working and to come up with new ideas."

I could feel sweat trickling down my back. *Keep going*, I told myself. *Be Pippi*.

"If we get the meeting, I'll talk first." Just saying those words made my stomach twist into a hundred knots, but I knew I had to be the one to start things off. "After that, I hope others will jump in and speak, too. And please remember, we're not going to name names. And we're not going to say all boys are bad, because they're not." I looked at Dion, wondering if he felt out of place. He just smiled and gave me a thumbs-up. If he felt strange, he didn't show it. I sure was glad he was there.

"This is about changing our school. Changing how we treat one another. Changing the way some of the boys think about girls. We just want things to be equal, you know?"

As everyone looked over the list, the librarian, Mrs. Thompson, motioned me over to her desk. The pit in my stomach was now the size of a basketball. Was she mad? Was I going to get in trouble? But she didn't say a thing.

She just handed me a piece of paper. I looked down and immediately recognized it. It was a haiku I had written not long after I'd started middle school. I'd stuck it in a book, and I guess Mrs. Thompson had found it.

One day, I will speak.
One day, I won't be afraid.
One day, things will change.

"Do you remember how you felt writing that?" she asked.

I nodded as I blinked back the tears.

"Carry that feeling with you today, Hazel," she said. "It's those kinds of powerful feelings that help change the world." She rubbed my back. "Because maybe one day is today."

CHAPTER THIRTY-NINE

There were probably a hundred of us. As we walked through the halls toward the principal's office, I felt so proud. I didn't know what would happen next, but one thing I did know? There was no going back now. Whatever happened, we wouldn't give up. I knew it as well as I knew that haiku made me happy.

A lot of the students were in the cafeteria eating. Others were in class since we have two lunch periods. One girl had told me she'd asked her teacher if it was okay to step out because she wanted to be with the students who were trying to talk to the principal. I'm sure some others ditched their classes so they could join us.

Tori walked beside me. "You ready for this?" she asked.

"I don't know, but I think we're about to find out."

She held my hand. "You got this. I know it. We're behind you."

I squeezed her hand. "I love your hopeful heart."

And I remembered what my mom had said. "If there are people around you who have your back, remember this moment, okay?" That moment when I hadn't been scared to say what I was thinking, about how things aren't exactly fair for girls. This was going to be like that, but with more people hearing the words, that was all.

I glanced behind me and saw an army of people who were with me. Mostly girls, but a few boys, too. Ben was in the crowd now, and he gave me a thumbs-up.

When we got to the office, we couldn't all fit, obviously, so a bunch stayed out in the hallway while the original seven who had planned to meet with the principal went inside. There were big glass windows around the office, so we could still see our entire group. And they could see us.

"We'd like to speak to Mr. Buck, please," Tori told the secretary.

"All of you?" she asked, motioning at the group outside.

Tori looked at me to answer. "If he wants, sure. But just us seven would be fine, too."

She stood up. "All right. Hold on."

She went down the little hallway where the principal and vice principal's offices were located. We watched as she disappeared behind a door. A minute later, she came back out.

"I'm sorry, he can't meet with you right now," she told us. "Are you Hazel, by chance?"

"Yes, that's me," I said.

"He said he told your mom he'd be happy to meet with the two of you. Why don't you have her set that up?"

"Because this isn't about just me," I told her. "It involves all of us."

"Well, he can't speak to all of you. It's not possible."

At those last three words, my heart dropped to my stomach. Everything I'd done to help get us here, all our excitement, all our work, and nothing would come of any of it? Without any changes at school, would the boys just start another notebook? Would things get worse instead of better if they learned they'd been caught but nothing had been done about it?

It couldn't end this way. It just couldn't.

"Um, is the vice principal in her office?" I asked.

"Ms. Carson?" she said. "Yes, she is. Why?"

"Could you maybe see if she might talk to us?"

The secretary didn't seem thrilled with the idea, but she turned around and went back down the hall. A minute later, Ms. Carson stepped out of her office. She's tall and wears teal glasses that I really love. She came right over to us and asked, "What's going on?"

"We wanted to talk to Mr. Buck, but he won't see us," I said. "Can you help?"

"He told me it's not possible to speak to so many students," the secretary tried to explain.

Ms. Carson said, "And why not?" But she didn't wait for an answer, probably because the secretary didn't exactly know why. Ms. Carson looked at Tori and me. "What's this about, exactly? Can you tell me?"

Before I could answer, Tori said, "We have a jerk problem at this school, and we're tired of it."

"Yes," I said. "And we have some ideas to make our school better, and we want to talk to Mr. Buck about them. Shouldn't he want to hear from us about the problems and some of the ideas we have to fix them?"

"Absolutely," she said. "Stay here. I'll be right back."

She turned around and marched down the hallway and into Mr. Buck's office.

"I wish I could hear what she's saying," Tori whispered to me.

"Me too," I said.

Outside the office, some of the kids were starting to get rowdy. I was trying to figure out what to say to them to let them know this wasn't the time to act like fidgety second graders. Fortunately, I didn't have to do anything. Maddie Gray stepped out of the group and told them they needed to be quiet for a couple more minutes; we were just waiting to get the meeting.

And that's about how long it was until Ms. Carson and Mr. Buck came back to speak to us.

Mr. Buck is a large and kinda scary man. He hardly ever smiles, though I guess being responsible for a few hundred middle school kids every day is probably hard. But seeing him coming toward us made me panic a little bit. Would I be able to speak without my voice shaking? Actually, would I be able to speak at all?

"Good afternoon, students," Mr. Buck said, his chest puffed out and his hands in his pockets. "Ms. Carson says you'd like to speak to me. I've got five minutes. Who wants to come into my office?"

I was about to gather the seven of us and step forward when Ms. Carson spoke up. "Actually, I bet we could have the library for a little while. Why don't we all go down there and anyone in the group who would like to stay is welcome?"

Mr. Buck turned and looked at Ms. Carson. "You sure that's a good idea?"

"Of course it is," she said with a smile. "Mary, can you please call Mrs. Thompson and let her know we're on our way?"

As the secretary picked up the phone, Ms. Carson stepped between Tori and me, then went through the office door and out into the hall. Mr. Buck followed behind her, his feet kind of shuffling. He did not look happy. Meanwhile, a lot of the people in our group looked like they wanted to do cartwheels down the hallway.

I couldn't believe it. We'd done it. We were going to get to speak with him!

Inside the library, some people sat at the twelve or so tables that are set up for classes to use while others stood back against the shelves. There's a podium and a projector at the front of the library where teachers stand and give lessons sometimes.

Ms. Carson stood next to Tori and me. "Why don't you join me at the podium," she told us. "Bring along anyone else who wants to speak as well."

I motioned to the others and we walked up to the front of the room. This wasn't what I'd expected at all. It was supposed to be the seven of us in a small room with the principal. This was like standing on a stage, giving a speech.

I told myself, *This is what we wanted.*

I told myself, *If I don't do this, a bunch of boys will get away with something horrible and nothing will change.*

I told myself to be like Pippi.

"Mr. Buck," I began.

"Louder, we can't hear you!" someone called from the back.

I cleared my voice and tried again. "Mr. Buck, we want to tell you about some things that have been going on at this school that you may not know about. I found a notebook with a bunch of girls' names. A notebook that boys were passing around to each other. Under each girl's name was a rating and comments about her looks. I brought the page with my name so you can see it." I pulled the folded piece of paper from my pocket and handed it to the principal.

"Imagine pages and pages like this. Imagine boys discussing girls like we're cattle or cars or something. We're human beings, and the way we look should be the least important part of who we are."

Now Tori moved up next to me to speak. "We have to change things at this school. The dress code that makes girls out to be the bad guys. The bullying that happens every day in our halls. And the way boys view us girls.

Because the way it is right now, it's not a fun place to be for a whole lot of us. And yeah, we get that school isn't supposed to be fun like a carnival or going to the mall or whatever. But we shouldn't hate coming here every day, should we?"

"All we want," I said, "is for people to treat us with kindness. With understanding. With respect."

And the entire library burst into applause.

TWO MONTHS LATER

CHAPTER FORTY

As Tori and I walked toward the gym, I checked out some of the new posters that had been hung on the walls that week. Someone had drawn a bunch of happy faces with the words BE THE REASON SOMEONE SMILES TODAY. Another person had drawn two hands reaching toward each other with a heart behind it. It said, BE A BUDDY, NOT A BULLY.

When I walked past Dion's poster, I smiled. I'd probably looked at it a hundred times and I never got tired of it. It said, WHEN YOU SEE SOMETHING BAD AND YOU SAY NOTHING, YOU'RE SAYING IT'S OKAY.

It wasn't a haiku, but it really spoke to me just the same. He'd drawn a girl sitting against a row of lockers, her knees curled up and her head in her hands. It reminded me of the day we'd found Dion in the library, crying against the bookshelf. I was so glad things had gotten better since then. Not perfect, obviously. Nothing's perfect. But better.

A couple of weeks ago, the principal had announced two winners of the poster contest, one of them Dion, who received gift cards for free frozen yogurt. Dion treated Tori and me on a Saturday afternoon. We'd laughed and laughed at how full Dion had made his cup of yogurt. He'd gotten some of each flavor and then piled on mini M&M'S. The gift card had been for twenty dollars, and I'm pretty sure his cup used up half of it.

"Tomorrow our class is discussing *Hidden Figures*," Tori said as we continued walking. "You finished it yet?"

"Yeah, we discussed it in my class yesterday," I said. "It was so good."

"I know, I loved it."

So far we'd had two books that the whole school had been assigned to read, and then each Language Arts teacher was responsible for having a discussion about it. I loved seeing everyone carrying around the same book. The teachers were working hard to choose books that would inspire us to be good humans while also helping us to see that women could do anything men could do.

Hidden Figures was about four African American women who were mathematicians and had worked for NASA. Without them, the United States would have taken a lot longer to launch a rocket into space. They'd done so much to help with the mission and had hardly gotten any credit for all their amazing work.

I'd written both Mr. Buck and Ms. Carson thank-you notes for agreeing to all three of our suggestions. At first, the boys had complained about going to training about toxic masculinity, since they thought it sounded insulting. But once it was over, I'd heard a lot of people talking about how good it'd been.

It wasn't about saying boys are bad, because they aren't. It showed us that a lot of it comes down to the way society treats boys and girls. We'd learned that even though the brains of boys and girls are practically the same, society treats us very differently. It happens from the minute we're born and that's the real problem. Like, why do so many shirts for baby girls have lollipops and cherries on them while boys get cars and trucks? Our instructor told us that it seems to her, just looking at baby clothes and the huge differences even then, that society is telling us girls should be cute enough to eat while boys are tough, tough, tough. And as kids grow, we don't let boys cry or girls get angry, and so they learn to feel shame when they have those natural feelings.

Sadly, nothing had changed as far as the dress code, but my parents and Tori's moms and some other parents were working on it. Mom told me, "Sometimes change happens quickly. And sometimes progress takes time. The important thing is to not give up. Just have to remember, anything is possible."

"Hey!" Dion said, running up behind us. "Wait up."

We turned around. He had fancy pants on with velvet along the sides along with the T-shirt my mom had bought that said, ALL YOU NEED IS LOVE, EQUAL RIGHTS, AND CUPCAKES.

Tori and I wore black circle skirts Alice had sewn for us,

perfect for dancing and twirling. Our T-shirts said MY BODY IS NONE OF YOUR BUSINESS.

"Sorry," Tori said. "We waited out front after our families went inside, but we were getting cold. Glad you found us. Since we aren't allowed to have cell phones backstage, our parents took them, so we couldn't text you."

"It's all right," he said. "Sorry I'm late. Grandma couldn't decide what to wear."

"Did you make sure her bra strap isn't showing?" Tori teased. "That's all that matters around here, you know."

We all laughed. Because sometimes, that's all you can do.

"Your parents and brother came, too, right?" I asked.

"Yep," he said. "I left them at the ticket taker and ran here to find you."

"They've all listened to us practice enough in the attic," I said. "They're probably glad to finally see it instead of just hear it."

"It's this way," Tori told us as she opened a set of double doors. "Probably shouldn't peek out at the audience. It'll just make us even more nervous."

"Yeah, okay," I told her as she led us up some stairs, down a hall, and into a big room backstage where all the students were hanging out. Some of them were stretching, some were warming up their vocals, and a few were tuning their instruments.

"I can't believe I'm doing this," I whispered. "Is it too late to change my mind?"

"Yes!" Tori and Dion said at the same time.

Then Dion told me, "If I can start dance class in a few weeks, then you can do this for five minutes."

I knew he was right.

Just then, a woman came by with a list. "Here's the order of the acts," she said. "We have a space marked right off-stage where the people can wait before it's their turn. That way, no one is scrambling and surprised when it's time for them to go on."

While she talked, I scanned the list for our names. We were the second ones to perform! Knowing I would be going out there very, very soon, my heart started to race.

True, things had gotten much better. For me. For other girls. For the entire school. But I still got nervous. And people still did and said mean things sometimes. That's just life, I guess. Two steps forward, one step back, as my mom had said so many times these past months as she continued to fight for the promotion she hadn't received. We didn't know how that would end, but one thing I did know? My mom was my hero, and I was so grateful for her help and support.

"Come on," Tori said, grabbing our hands and pulling us toward the waiting area offstage.

We stood behind three boys who were going to perform a skit. We'd seen it during practice, and it was pretty funny. It seemed like a good way to start off the show. Laughter always puts people in a good mood.

Ms. Carson went up to the microphone and thanked everyone for coming. She told them she was excited we were showcasing all the amazing talent at our school. "We've gone through a bit of a transformation these past couple of months," she said. "A transformation powered by students. And I've never been prouder to work here. So let's give these kids a big round of applause and get started with the show!"

Next, the drama teacher, Ms. Franklin, introduced herself and told everyone the names of the boys in the first act. Then we watched them do their funny skit about camping. The audience roared with laughter and clapped really hard when they finished.

The three of us looked at one another. Tori whispered, "We got this."

When we stepped out onstage, a flash of memories came at me all at once. All the things that had happened that helped me to be here now, standing next to my amazing friends.

Finding the notebook.

Meeting Pip.

Meeting Dion.

Stealing the notebook.

Loving Pip.

Seeing Pip scared.

Seeing me in Pip.

Realizing I could hide or stick my neck out.

Giving Pip up so others could learn from him.

Finding strength in others.

Standing up.

Speaking out.

Months ago, I couldn't have imagined myself on this stage. It had seemed impossible for me. But here I was. Here we were.

I repeated Tori's words to myself. *We got this.*

As the music started, the three of us stepped side to side and then spun around, just like we'd practiced. The audience clapped right away!

We'd found a video on YouTube of three girls signing this particular song for a college sign language class. No joke, I'd probably watched it a hundred times, at least. Those girls made it look so easy and it wasn't at all, but thanks to them, it was easier than it would have been.

As Tori belted out the lyrics for Aretha Franklin's song "Respect," my hands and Dion's hands signed the words. I looked out and saw people bobbing their heads and snapping their fingers. It seemed like everyone was smiling. Everyone.

When she got to the words, "All I'm asking is for a little respect," I swear I got goose bumps all over my body.

We'd stuck our necks out for some respect. And it had worked.

Maybe, just maybe, adults weren't the only ones with superpowers, after all.

ACKNOWLEDGMENTS

A big thank you to the girls at Bethesda-Chevy Chase High School in Bethesda, Maryland, who made the news and inspired this story. You stood up to the toxic culture at your high school and helped make change happen. While I'm grateful for the story inspiration, I'm even more grateful for your conviction and courage.

I also want to thank the educators who work tirelessly day in and day out to make school a safe place for everyone. It's not easy, I know, but it's important, and those of you who realize that and do the necessary work deserve recognition and appreciation.

Finally, thank you to my editor, Amanda Maciel, and the teams at Scholastic, Scholastic Book Clubs, and Scholastic Book Fairs for your support over the years!

ABOUT THE AUTHOR

Lisa Schroeder is the author of twenty books for young readers, including *See You on a Starry Night, Wish on All the Stars, Keys to the City, Sealed with a Secret, My Secret Guide to Paris*, and the Charmed Life series. She loves tea and cookies, flowers, family hikes, books and movies that make her laugh and cry, and sunshine. Living in Oregon, she doesn't get nearly enough sunshine, but the hikes are amazing. You can visit her online at lisaschroederbooks.com and on Instagram at @lisaschroeder15.

On a starry night, anything is possible . . .

See You on a Starry Night

LISA
SCHROEDER

Turn the page for more from Lisa Schroeder!

Casper, my old, white kitty, sat perched on my nightstand, studying me like I might unpack a can of tuna any second. Poor cat. No tuna here; just all of the moving boxes marked "Juliet."

"Sweet kitty, I'm sorry, but you have to move." I picked him up and kissed the top of his head before placing him on my green and purple striped quilt. Then I reached into the practically empty box and pulled out a framed family photo taken at my eleventh birthday party last August.

As I put the photo down in its spot right next to my bed, I studied it and felt a pinch in my chest. Mom, Dad, my older sister Miranda, and I all wore pointy red and blue hats and had party horns in our mouths. The picture captures a short minute of a long day. Besides making me feel pretty ridiculous, the hat's elastic strap had dug into my chin a little, so I hadn't worn it long. None of my friends had either. They'd put them on for a picture before we started eating, then taken them right back off again. I'd only bought them because Dad had practically insisted on the hats and the horns when we went to the party store for invitations.

When Mom had shown me the photo, I couldn't believe how happy we all looked. I asked if I could have a copy framed.

Now I loved it even more, because not only had we been happy, but we'd also been together—a family. I'd have worn one of those silly blue and red hats every day if it meant we didn't have to move away from everything I'd ever loved.

Some wishes are bigger than others . . .

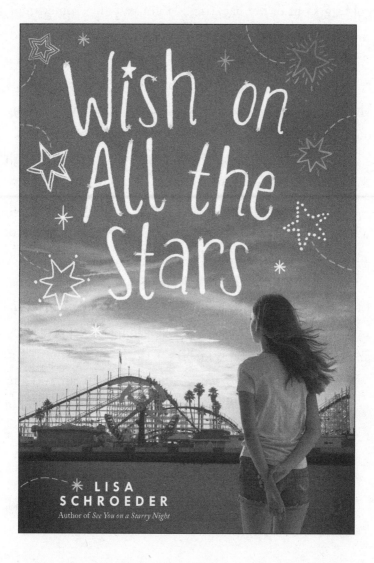

Turn the page for more from Lisa Schroeder!

Emma pulled a small, red gift bag splattered with blue and gold stars out of her backpack. "I got you guys something," she told us, her green eyes twinkling like stars as she smiled.

I stared at the bag, wondering what it could be. She reached in and pulled out three little boxes wrapped in baby blue tissue paper. "One for you, Juliet," she said, pushing one toward me. "One for you, Carmen. And one for me."

"I love that you wrapped one for yourself, even though you know what it is," Carmen said.

"Would've ruined the surprise if I didn't," she said. "Okay, on the count of three, let's open them. One. Two. Three."

I carefully tore the tissue paper and opened my box. Inside was a teensy tiny bottle with a note rolled up inside it. I picked up the bottle and saw that it hung on a pretty silver chain. "Oh my gosh," I said. "It's perfect!"

As we all went to work attaching them around our necks, I asked, "Did you write us notes on the tiny pieces of paper using your best tiny handwriting?"

"No, but you can pretend I did," she replied.

"What would you have written?" Carmen asked.

"Um . . ." She thought for a moment. "I would have said, 'Always remember, wishes do come true.'"